Enrollment Form

☐ *Yes!* I WANT TO BE A *Privileged Woman.*

Enclosed is one *PAGES & PRIVILEGES*™ Proof of Purchase
from any Harlequin or Silhouette book currently for
sale in stores (Proofs of Purchase are found on
the back pages of books) and the store cash
register receipt. Please enroll me in *PAGES
& PRIVILEGES*™. Send my Welcome
Kit and FREE Gifts -- and activate my
FREE benefits -- immediately.

*More great gifts and benefits to come like these
luxurious Truly Lace and L'Effleur gift baskets.*

NAME (please print)

ADDRESS   APT. NO

CITY   STATE   ZIP/POSTAL CODE

PROOF OF PURCHASE *SAMPLE ONLY*

Please allow 6-8 weeks for delivery. Quantities are
limited. We reserve the right to substitute items.
Enroll before October 31, 1995 and receive
one full year of benefits.

NO CLUB!
NO COMMITMENT!

*Just one purchase brings
you great* **Free Gifts**
and **Benefits!**

(More details in back of this book.)

Name of store where this book was purchased_____

Date of purchase_____

Type of store:

☐ Bookstore   ☐ Supermarket   ☐ Drugstore

☐ Dept. or discount store (e.g. K-Mart or Walmart)

☐ Other (specify)_____

Which Harlequin or Silhouette series do you usually read?
_____

Pages
& Privileges™

Complete and mail with one Proof of Purchase and store receipt to:

U.S.: *PAGES & PRIVILEGES*™, P.O. Box 1960, Danbury, CT 06813-1960

Canada: *PAGES & PRIVILEGES*™, 49-6A The Donway West, P.O. 813,
North York, ON M3C 2E8   **PRINTED IN U.S.A**

Dear Reader,

When I first saw my newborn daughter, Meagan, I was scared half to death. This was a life I created and I could lose her in the bedclothes! I was afraid to hold her, change her or feed her, and left all that to her mother, worshiping the tiny thing from a distance.

But necessity has a way of making you grow. When Meagan's mother left us, I was forced into learning all the everyday things about the child I'd created. It was just as tough on Meagan as it was on me. We learned together how to get dressed, eat with a spoon and when to take naps. I had to absorb so much and became just as frustrated as any on-the-job mother.

But I also realized what most mothers experience and not too many men ever know: that there is nothing so wonderful as giving a child all your love and care, and having it returned in trust and devotion, shown in the light of big, innocent eyes and a hand just big enough to wrap trustingly around your finger.

Beau McGuire

Please address questions and book requests to: Harlequin Reader Service
U.S.: 3010 Walden Ave., P.O. Box 1325, Buffalo, NY 14269
Canadian: P.O. Box 609, Fort Erie, Ont. L2A 5X3

RITA CLAY ESTRADA

THE BEST THINGS IN LIFE

Harlequin Books

TORONTO • NEW YORK • LONDON
AMSTERDAM • PARIS • SYDNEY • HAMBURG
STOCKHOLM • ATHENS • TOKYO • MILAN
MADRID • WARSAW • BUDAPEST • AUCKLAND

To Marilyn Staggs, a longtime friend who always takes the time to listen—or to talk—whichever comes first.

To Jean Weisner, for a terrific sense of humor and for being a good friend.

And to Kay Garteiser, who has so much goodness in her heart that it overflows to the rest of us.

Let's all meet at I. H., and I'll buy the first round of drinks.

HARLEQUIN BOOKS
225 Duncan Mill Road, Don Mills,
Ontario, Canada M3B 3K9

ISBN 0-373-88515-6

THE BEST THINGS IN LIFE

Copyright © 1986 by Rita Clay Estrada

1

CLENCHING HIS big, well-manicured hands, Beau McGuire banged them repeatedly against the windowsill in Len's office while he waited tensely for the phone to ring. He stared out, unseeing, at the misty New York skyline. His back was rigid, his muscles wire-tight, his whole frame straining to hear a telephone ring that didn't come.

Behind him, Len sat at his enormous cherry wood desk twirling a pencil while his own eyes were riveted to the phone as if compelling it to ring. Beau was grateful Len was there. He wasn't just the talented director of the top-rated soap opera Beau starred in; Len was also a close friend. And Beau needed someone to wait with him right now. He stared out the thirty-eighth-story window, as if his little daughter Meagan might appear in front of it at any minute. Dear Lord, if only she would . . .

Len cleared his throat, challenging the strained silence. "When did she kidnap Meagan?"

Beau jerked his head toward him. "Four days ago. My sister wasn't home when she came, just the housekeeper. When Pamela asked if she could just take Meagan for an ice-cream cone and would bring her right back, the woman believed her. But dear Pamela left a note right next to the phone—demanding money or she wouldn't return Meagan."

Sighing, Beau tried to control the panic welling in him. "That's when I screwed up. When . . . when she called, I really let her have it, threatening her with a prison term if she didn't return Meagan immediately. I must have scared the hell out of her, because the next thing I know, her boyfriend is calling me a maniac and hanging up. They've been on the run ever since, with the private detective right behind them."

Eyes darkened with hatred and frustrated at his inability to do anything but wait, Beau growled, "If anything happens to Meagan, I swear I'll kill that black-hearted bitch!"

Len leaned back in his expensive leather swivel chair and rubbed his eyes. "You've kept this to yourself all this time? You must have been going crazy! I don't know how you managed to work with this nightmare hanging over your head."

Beau ran visibly shaking fingers through his midnight-dark hair. "What could I do? The police are trying in their unique red-tape way, but they don't think parental kidnapping is as serious a crime as others. In fact, it's even considered a civil matter, not criminal, since the people involved are both parents."

"But it's kidnapping!" Len exclaimed.

Beau swallowed hard before he could speak. He had repeated the same response to a hundred people. "I know, but the police's hands are tied. There's a whole new set of laws every time the three of them cross another state line. And a new set of rules. Thank goodness for Lewell, the private detective who's been keeping me informed every step of the way, or I'd go totally out of my mind."

"My God," Len whispered.

Beau faced into the room, knowing his eyes revealed stark fear and desolation, but he was unable to hide his feelings. "I don't think Pamela would hurt Meagan, but I don't trust the creep she's with. He's a worthless bum—and he has my daughter!"

"You'll be written out of the script by tomorrow," Len reminded him. "After that you'll have as much free time as you need to find her."

"Thanks," Beau said, but he hadn't really been listening. He knew Len had done what he asked; he just couldn't seem to remember anything except that Meagan was no longer with him. Not in his arms, his house or under his protection. He literally ached from the absence of her small body in his heart and his home.

Len sat up straight and arched his back as if to ease a twinge. "As you said, Pamela might not be the best, most stable woman on earth, but she *is* Meagan's mother. She must have some feelings for Meagan. Besides, no normal person would harm a three-year-

old." All evening long Len had been mouthing these
encouraging platitudes. That one only added to the
mounting total, and they both knew it.

Beau closed his eyes for a moment. "I still can't believe Pamela would do such a thing to her own
daughter! I knew she was selfish, but I never expected
this from her. Never." He turned back to stare out at
the late-evening rain that dribbled down the panes,
magnifying and blurring the skyline into a shimmer
of colored carnival lights. He refused to consider the
fact that he might never see Meagan again. "Pamela
had better be the perfect mother until I catch up with
her or her days are numbered." His voice was low and
measured, but the meaning that knifed the stillness of
the room was vividly clear.

His eyes flicked toward the ceiling for a moment as
he tried to regain control. How could any mother steal
her own child away from the only security and love
she had known her entire life and hold her for ransom?

Try as he could, he simply couldn't understand Pamela, but then that wasn't new. Hell, she had will-
ingly turned the child over to Beau before Meagan was
even born, guaranteeing that she wouldn't have to be
responsible for her child. However, soon after Meagan's birth Pamela had filed a custody suit against him
using the very money he had paid her to seek a new
life for herself. Eventually they had settled out of
court, with Beau retaining custody, after she had ex-

tracted some more money from him. "To begin a new life," she had said.

That was what got him most. All the agony he was going through, all Meagan was going through, was only for money. A few more bucks so Pamela and her ratty boyfriend could start over somewhere.

The hurt deep in his chest swelled until he wanted to scream from it. Instead, he sucked in a long, painful breath and watched the rain streaking the dirty window.

IT WAS ALMOST THREE O'CLOCK in the morning when Honey Carter first heard the child wail from the rear of her fern-green van.

She had been to one of those compulsory parties her best client gave once a year and had stayed as long as she could stand to. When she had finally slipped away, the party was still going strong. It was business, so she had remained longer than she really wanted to. Then, after saying good-night to her tipsy host, she had walked for a block to clear the cigarette smoke from her lungs and to get rid of the pungent smell of liquor and the cloying mixture of too many perfumes before strolling back to her van and heading for home.

Now parked in the garage of her rural home and listening to what sounded like the pitiful whimper of a small child, Honey felt the hair on the back of her neck rise.

She spun around, one hand reaching for the interior light switch. Her large, plush van was suddenly bathed in brilliant light, and the seated figure of a tiny dark-haired girl was clearly outlined against the pale green velvet of the full-width back seat. Her wailing ceased instantly. Big green eyes stared at Honey, as surprised as she was that someone should be in the van. The tattered remnant of a yellow blanket was clutched in one chubby fist, and a faded gray bunny, minus one ear, dangled from the other.

Honey didn't know much about kids, but judging from her size, this one couldn't have been more than three or four, and the child seemed to be as frightened of Honey as she had been of the child.

"Good grief, what have we here?" she muttered, running a hand through the shoulder-length hair that had supplied her nickname.

At the sound of Honey's voice, the child began to whimper again, moving to one corner of the seat as if to distance herself from the strange woman who was staring so hard at her.

Then Honey noticed the yellow satchel on the padded van floor, along with what was obviously a note attached by a big safety pin.

Honey's eyes darted back to the small bundle curled up on the couch, swathed in a worn pink nightgown. She looked like a De Grazia painting of an Indian infant, all big round eyes and roly-poly body. She continued to whimper softly.

Honey's heart, already pounding in double time, constricted unwillingly at the sound. "Oh, darling, don't cry," she crooned, swivelling out of the captain's seat and moving toward the child, her arms open wide in anticipation. "I don't know how you got here or what I'm going to do with you, but I promise I won't bite," she said, trying to calm the child, who was looking at her as if she were the wicked witch of fairy tales.

Honey melted at the sight of the crystalline tears that had streaked down dirt-smudged cheeks to the child's tiny chin. She felt as if she had been kicked in the stomach, as if the pain the child obviously felt was hers, too.

"Oh, my God," she whispered in the sudden silence. Her hand gently touched the little girl's blue-black ringlets. But it was the stoic, defeated look in the child's bright green eyes that hurt Honey the most. Her heart squeezed with pain at the stark fear the little girl was feeling.

Slowly, ever so slowly, she enfolded the child into the comfort of her arms, cradling her with a tenderness she hadn't known she was capable of. After a split second of hesitation, the child rested against her breast as if she had consciously decided to trust the tall honey-haired woman. Honey barely held back her own tears at the gesture.

She rocked the little girl gently, finally allowing a few pent-up tears to roll down her cheeks and plop on the child's hair. "Poor, sweet baby," she murmured. "Poor, sweet baby."

The eerie, hollow sound of a horn carried faintly through the carpeted sides of the van. In the distance, a dog decided to answer the clarion with a howl of its own. Then silence returned.

Honey's eyes fastened on the note. Leaning forward, she squinted to make out the scrawled handwriting.

Please take care of Meagan until her father can be reached. I can't cope with her anymore.

Scribbled on the bottom was a man's name, Beau McGuire, and telephone number with a New York area code. Honey recognized the area code because she had an old school friend who lived in New York.

"Well, Meagan McGuire," she whispered into the stillness, one hand brushing back coal-black locks from the child's forehead, "it looks like you and I are going to be bedmates for the night." She glanced at her watch before smiling tenderly at the girl. "It's already after three o'clock, and I don't think your daddy can make it here until tomorrow afternoon. It's past four in the morning, his time."

She scooped the chubby bundle into her arms and carried the child out of her side door of the van. Walking carefully around to the driver's side, she reached in, opened her purse and hooked it over her shoulder while she felt for her house keys.

For the past three years she had lived alone in this large, rambling house on the northwestern outskirts of Houston. She ran her bookkeeping and accounting service from there and very rarely traveled far from home. Why should she? Everything she wanted was inside the boundaries of her ten acres.

With a bit of juggling, Honey finally managed to get the back door of the house open. Meagan's hands were looped around her neck, her baby-soft cheek on Honey's shoulder. She wouldn't ease her tight grip, although her whimpering had stopped at last.

Honey gave her a slight squeeze. The protective feelings for this child curled in her arms made Honey feel warm all over. She grimaced inwardly at her own maternal instincts shoving so hard to the fore. What in heaven's name did she know about children? Nothing! They had to be fed and cleaned, but beyond that it was all a mystery. Well, common sense would have to suffice.

Closing the door and giving the lock a twist, she shifted the burden in her arms, then flicked on the kitchen lights. Their hold on each other was awkward, but neither one would relinquish it. She dropped Meagan's bag and her own purse onto the round butcher-block table.

Now what? Probably something to eat or drink first. A plastic glass for a child made sense. Propping Meagan on one hip, Honey reached for the cabinet door. Proud of herself for thinking so logically, she

filled a sunshine-yellow plastic tumbler to the brim
with milk, then held it up to Meagan's bow lips. Meagan took several deep gulps before pushing it away to
snuggle back into the secure hollow of Honey's slender body.

So much for thirst.

Now what?

"Potty?" Meagan asked, and Honey's eyes lit with
delight at the beautiful doll's first word. It might not
have looked too classy carved in stone, but the question was basic and directly to the point.

"You bet, darlin'," Honey murmured, walking
down the hall and into the bathroom. Another awkward moment. It took a great deal of calm and inge-
nuity for her to balance a small child just right, but it
worked. Feeling terribly proud of her achievement,
Honey washed Meagan's face and hands and then
carried the child into the bedroom, turning on the
lights as she went. Even if Honey had wanted to put
the small bundle into the guest room, she didn't think
the child would feel secure or stay there. Her bed was
as good a place to sleep as any. Thank goodness it was
queen-sized.

Unbidden thoughts popped in her head like heat-
exploded kernels of corn, but she shoved them away
just as quickly. First things first. Right now she had to
get Meagan to sleep before she could concentrate on
contacting her father. She ignored the little voice that
told her she should have called him immediately, then

had someone in authority come and take the child off her hands. Logic told her that that was the correct choice; her emotional self ignored it totally.

Talking to Meagan in a soothing tone, Honey pulled down the heavy comforter and sheets, then laid the toddler in the center of the bed. She tucked her in, then paused, as if held by some force she wasn't aware of, and smoothed the dark curls away from the child's face. One grimy paw of the one-eared gray rabbit was showing, and the tattered blanket was clutched in Meagan's other fist.

An overwhelming anger swelled almost to bursting in Honey's breast as she pondered the nature of a person who could just dump a child. What kind of vile animal was the woman that could do that? And what had she meant when she'd written she couldn't "cope with her anymore"?

Meagan's eyelids closed, fluttered, then closed again, and with a shallow child's sigh, she slipped into a deep sleep.

Almost reluctantly, Honey tiptoed from the room, closing the door until just a crack of dim light showed. Could children cry loud enough to be heard through a closed door? She didn't know, but she didn't want to take any chances.

Now to the yellow case.

Loud-colored plastic, it was the kind that could be picked up in any discount store. But this one was slightly different. It was torn on one side from one diagonal corner to the other. Honey handled the case gingerly, as if there were germs crawling all over it.

Inside were a pair of name-brand turquoise shorts with a coordinated striped top and a pair of expensive tan leather sandals. Digging into the bottom of the case, she found, in shining splendor, an oval tortoiseshell hairbrush inlaid with hammered silver. She picked it up to examine it more closely. Sterling.

"Well, I'll be," she said softly, studying the object in her hand. What in the world was an abandoned child doing with such an expensive hairbrush? For that matter, how could the mother afford the costly sandals and clothing, yet dress her child in a nightgown that looked like it had been picked up at a garage sale? Nothing made sense.

Unhooking the duck's head diaper pin, she read the note again. The father's name was Beau McGuire. Stifling a yawn, Honey checked her watch. It was almost four o'clock, almost five New York time—just as good a time as any.

She picked up the phone and punched the numbers, ignoring the small butterflies cavorting in the pit of her stomach. What would she say? How would she possibly explain this bizarre situation? *Mr. McGuire, I found your child in the back of my van in Houston. She's exhausted and frightened. Would you please come and get her?*

The phone rang: two, three, four, five times. No answer. Her brow furrowed. Where would a grown man be at this time of the morning if he wasn't asleep?

When the phone was finally answered, there was a woman's voice at the other end of the line. Groggy, muffled, but definitely female.

"Hello?"

So much for the harried father's concern for the welfare of his child. He was probably in bed with a—

"Hello, is Mr. McGuire there, please?"

"Pamela? Is that you?" Now the voice was wide awake. "Answer me, dammit! Where are you?"

"This isn't Pamela," Honey answered patiently, silently irritated by the woman's accusatory hysterics. "I'm calling long-distance for Mr. Beau McGuire. May I speak to him, please?"

"Who is this?" the other woman demanded.

"This is Honey Carter from Houston, but I doubt if my name will ring any bells for him." She took a deep breath, promising herself not to let this woman irk her further. She had a job to do, then she could get to sleep. "I repeat, is Mr. Beau McGuire there?"

"He's not here," the woman answered. "And I suggest you not call again. Mr. McGuire doesn't like his fans calling on his private line. How did you get this number, anyway?"

"When will he return?" Honey just kept charging ahead. Somehow she knew she had to get the information she needed before she could give out the information she had.

"If I were you, I wouldn't try calling back. Mr. McGuire will only hang up on you. If you must get in touch with him, call his secretary at the studio or send a fan letter, but leave his private number alone."

The phone clicked in Honey's ear.

Lost in thought, she leaned back, replaying the conversation. What studio and what fans was the woman talking about? She went over the name again in her mind. Beau McGuire. Beau McGuire. It sounded familiar, but maybe she was merely getting used to the name.

Stifling a yawn, Honey rose and walked slowly out of the kitchen and climbed the stairs to the bedroom, turning out lights as she went. She'd wait until later to call again. Perhaps then Mr. McGuire himself would answer and she could get this business over with.

But right now she had to sleep.

She unfastened her dress and shrugged it onto the floor. Shoes and panty hose were next. Glancing toward the form curled into a tight little ball in her bed, she frowned. Was it too cold, too hot? Did the child have enough room? She shook her head, not knowing any of the answers and too tired to figure them out. She crawled into bed without bothering to wash her face or change into pajamas. An ecru slip and lace panties were enough of a concession, especially since she was so darn tired.

Unconsciously she reached over to tuck the sheet a little higher under the child's chin, then patted it into place. Closing her eyes, Honey drifted into a dreamless sleep. She wasn't aware when the small figure snuggled her little bottom into the curve of Honey's body, cuddling deeply into the covers, but she felt the warmth of human touch and slept all the better for it.

"SHELLY, WAKE UP! Who called while I was in the shower?" Beau's voice was low-pitched but laced with impatience as he twitched his sister's foot to wake her.

Sleepy green eyes, almost identical to his, peered up before closing once more.

"Shelly, wake up!"

"Okay, okay. You don't have to shout," she complained, sitting up and brushing her hair out of her eyes. The clock in the living room chimed six and, with a groan, she slid down into the coziness of the covers. "It was just a fan of yours," she mumbled. "It wasn't Pamela."

"Are you sure? Did she say her name? Tell you why she was calling?" His forehead was lined with worry.

"It was just some fan who wanted to talk to you," his sister went on sleepily. "I told her to call your secretary at the studio or write you a fan letter, but not to bother you here."

Beau turned away in frustration, his broad shoulders momentarily blocking the soft, gray light that had begun to filter through the window. "Great! Besides a missing daughter, now I have a sister who aggravates my fans. Good grief, Shelly, use a little diplomacy, will you? Those fans pay my salary!"

A muffled grunt floated out from under the covers. "Huh! Your super acting pays your salary, not some woman who calls in the middle of the night."

He wiggled her foot again, fond exasperation for his "baby" sister showing plainly on his face. "I need you to stay close to the phone this morning, if you can. I'm expecting to hear from that private detective and I want you to transfer the call to the studio. He thinks he may have a lead on Pamela's destination."

A green eye peeked from beneath the covers. At last she was wide awake. "Really?"

Beau turned toward his sister, but his mind was already elsewhere. "Really. He called Len's office last night with the news. He traced them to Austin, Texas, but his partner lost their trail yesterday. He thinks her boyfriend is from a small coastal town and that they might be headed there."

"Is she alone, Beau? Or is she still traveling with that creep?"

"She's still with him." His voice was low, trembling from the agony of waiting and wondering, picturing his tiny daughter at the mercy of a mother who used her only child as bait for money. He had never felt so helpless. His hands were tied by the law and by his own inability to take part in the action. The only thing he could do was be patient and pray the detective would find Meagan before her mother could scar her mentally for life. His hands clenched in the pose he had taken so automatically in the past few days: fists that ached to punch something, someone, to obliterate the pain that wracked his thoughts.

Then he took a deep breath and moved to the door. "I'll be at the studio all morning, but I'll be back later this afternoon. Len's arranged to have me written out of the script."

"For good?" Shelly squeaked, alarm clearly displayed in her shocked expression.

"Don't worry. It's just until I get Meagan back and can make sure she's all right," he reassured her, his voice almost muffled by the distance. He was already at the front door of the luxury Fifth Avenue apartment. "And *that* had better be soon, or I'll go crazy!" He slammed the door as if to punctuate his outburst.

Briskly he strode down the hall, heading for the elevator. After punching the button, he stood, hands thrust in his pockets, as he impatiently waited for the sounds that meant the elevator was on its way up.

He still couldn't quite believe it. Five days ago Meagan had been a happy, secure three-year-old who knew no one's care except his sister's. She was somewhat shy, but Beau hadn't worried about that, realizing she was going through a phase. Meagan was growing up so quickly. Next week she was to have started nursery school three days a week.

The elevator doors slid open, and he stepped inside, pushing the lobby button and leaning against the wall, eyes closed.

For the past year he had been thinking that, for Meagan's sake, he should move to Long Island, or even to Connecticut, even though it meant he would have to commute. She needed green grass and tall trees and more room to play. She should have fresh air, and a bike that she could ride around garden paths, instead of marching around and around the living room couch. Everything had been going according to plan until four days ago when his world had begun spinning crazily. Pamela had always had that effect on him, but this time it wasn't out of love or infatuation. This time it was cold-blooded kidnapping.

Meagan *was* his world—the only important thing in his life, except for his work, and Pamela knew that only too well. She needed to have a normal childhood in order to grow up healthy and confident and become the kind of adult they could all be proud of. She already had one strike against her: only one true parent . . . and her father instead of her mother.

The police had been little or no help. Even though Beau had legal custody of Meagan, Pamela was the child's natural mother, and the police could see no reason to pursue the case with any zeal. Apparently not even the law would believe that a mother would harm her own child. Beau and Shelly knew better.

The elevator opened onto the small, elegant lobby, and Beau stepped out quickly, his footsteps echoing on the marble. He made his way out of the building and hailed a cab.

"National Studios," he said as he slid into the back seat. Sighing, he rested his head against the window as he stared out. New York City. The Big Apple. He and Shelly had been born on Long Island in Wantagh, a small town wryly nicknamed the "Gateway to Jones Beach." When he had just turned twelve and Shelly was five, their parents had been killed in a commuter train accident. That tragedy was the first in a series of blows the two had had to adjust to.

They had moved in with their mother's brother, a crusty, set-in-his-way bachelor who lived in Manhattan and operated a small but lucrative musical instrument rental store. What he knew about children could have been stuffed in the end of a flute. Music was his life, and he expected everyone else to appreciate it as he did. That was only one of many sore points. He also insisted on complete and total obedience, and tolerated no "errors." For a young boy growing into adolescence the experience was horrible, but for a small, cuddly girl who needed love and a woman's guiding hand, it was pure murder.

By the time Beau was in high school, he was working nights at any job he could get: washing dishes, sweeping out theaters, cleaning storefront windows. His big break came when he was hired as a page by one of the network television studios. He knew he had found his niche at last.

When the cab rounded a corner and passed Rockefeller Center, he smiled in recollection. He had worked at NBC for a year before landing a silly bit part in a commercial chewing gum while kicking up his heels on a skateboard. It had taken all day to film his tiny segment, but even after twenty takes he was hooked. He had left his uncle's home cheerfully to move in with five other guys in a room barely fit for one. Shelly had cried when he'd left, but he had promised he'd be back for her. And he had lived up to his promise after Pamela had charged into his life and turned it upside down.

He'd been a struggling actor when he'd first met her. She'd been sweet and dark-haired and had had the face of an angel. But she'd had no morals. She had proven that over and over again as Beau had become more involved with his career. Looking back again, he realized her behavior had merely been a way of getting his attention. When he had finally broken off with her, Pamela had threatened suicide. For three months they had tried to patch up the relationship, Beau attempting to recreate something he had soon realized wasn't there to begin with. He had wanted love, security and a home so badly he had overlooked most of Pamela's problems, distracted by her angelic features, sweet smile and innocent eyes.

Logically he'd known it was over for good, but his heart hadn't acknowledged that fact. They hadn't been working out, but he'd loved her anyway. That had been the hard part: knowing they were skidding on a downhill course and there was nothing he could do to stop it. The memory still hurt.

Then Pamela had discovered she was pregnant. Because of their attempts to reconcile, Beau had been sure the baby was his. With a heart burdened with the knowledge of a dying relationship but lightened by the exhilaration of impending fatherhood, he had literally bought his own baby. He had moved Pamela into an nearby apartment, making sure she ate correctly and taking her to the obstetrician for regular checkups.

Afterward had come her sporadic visits to gush over Meagan and dash off within an hour, bored by the baby and even more by Beau's fascination with their child. After the first two years, there had been no more visits.

Until now. She had crashed into his and Meagan's life with a bang, kidnapping the child she had sworn she hadn't wanted to bear in the first place.

His cab pulled up to the curb in front of the studio. After paying the man, Beau stepped out, glancing up at the patches of blue sky visible between the tall, glittering skyscrapers. The sun was already beginning to warm the concrete. It was going to be a beautiful spring day.

Passing quickly through the revolving doors, he signed in and flipped open his wallet to show his pass to the elevator guard before taking a car up to the thirty-eighth floor.

Pamela's latest escapade was hard on him. But it was hard on Shelly, too.

His sister had helped take care of Meagan ever since he had brought her home from the hospital—a tiny bundle of curly black hair, bright green laughing eyes and lungs that could emulate an ape call that rivaled Tarzan. He grinned sadly in reminiscence. She'd been loud when she was little, astounding him with her noise. But she'd never called out unless she was hungry or wet or uncomfortable. Shelly, too, had been amazed at what a good baby she was.

A sophomore at Hunter College when Meagan was born, Shelly had moved right in, cut back her class schedule and taken over Meagan's care when Beau was working. She continued at Hunter, working part-time on her teaching degree. They had made a pact. When Shelly got her degree, Beau would help her get settled so she could concentrate on her own career. Until then, she helped with Meagan, practicing what she learned in college and using Meagan as a kind of human guinea pig.

Beau knew that Shelly's patient lessons were one of the major reasons Meagan was so advanced for her age. Shelly took extra time and showed endless forbearance with the little girl, and she literally bloomed under her aunt's caring tutelage.

For Shelly, too, the days were empty without Meagan to care for, to laugh with. To hug . . . to love.

The elevator doors slid open, and Beau stepped out. It was time for work. He whispered a quick prayer that Meagan would soon be found.

HONEY'S EYES OPENED SLOWLY at first, blinking furiously against the light pouring through the uncurtained window. She didn't stir. Her muscles were sore and stiff, her mind clouded. What had made her feel so worn out?

Everything came back with a rush.

The party. The late night. The child.

Meagan lay curled against her, the girl's little rump snuggling closely into the lap Honey's bent legs formed. Her dark, shiny curls capped her head closely, her sooted lashes lying like dark shadows on her soft, baby-smooth skin. One chubby hand was thrown over her head to rest on the pillow, cupped slightly but relaxed. She was adorable, like one of those children in ads for tissue and detergents. Again the big question popped into Honey's head. What would make a mother abandon her child in a stranger's van?

Slowly, carefully, Honey eased away from the sleeping form. A faint whisper escaped from the child, but she wriggled her round bottom, one, twice, then settled again into a deep sleep.

Without bothering with her robe, Honey headed for the bedroom door. Once more she closed it all but a crack and slipped quietly down the stairs to the kitchen, intent on making coffee before trying to sort out her thoughts. She had all day to decide what to do with her wee houseguest. For some reason she was reluctant to admit, Honey knew she wasn't going to call in the authorities. First she'd find out what the father wanted her to do.

Funny, but for the past three years she had treasured her privacy, liked being on her own without anyone pestering her—her own personal brand of peace.

She turned on the portable radio on the windowsill, not really hearing the music or the farm reports given. A rare early-spring hurricane had turned toward the Texas coast. It had been spinning around out in the Gulf like a mother hen ready to hatch a prized egg. But Honey ignored the storm warning, too.

An image of Meagan as she looked in bed slipped into Honey's thoughts. She, who had never had a child, had never so much as considered adopting one, was firmly ensnared by two chubby arms, a pair of big, bright green eyes and a cap of runaway black curls.

She slammed the coffeepot down. All right! Enough of that! This child was not hers and must be returned to her father. As soon as that elusive man could be found!

Without hesitation, Honey turned and began to dial the number on the note. As the call was going through, she glanced at the round battery-operated clock hanging above the kitchen cabinets. Nine-thirty. Ten-thirty in New York. Someone should be home by now besides the sleeping beauty who had answered the phone before.

"McGuire residence." The voice was smooth, professional and female. A different one, though.

"May I speak to Mr. Beau McGuire, please."

"He's not in. May I tell him who called?"

Honey ignored the question. "When will he be in?"

"Mr McGuire doesn't usually return until late. But he will be calling in. May I forward your message?"

A very efficient woman. "Look, ma'am. This is an urgent personal matter and I must speak to Mr. McGuire. Where can he be reached?" Honey's patience was exhausted. Couldn't the man even answer his own phone, for heaven's sake? Didn't he care that his child was with a stranger? She wondered if he was even bothering to look for her.

"You could try reaching him through his secretary at the studio," the woman suggested. "He's usually there all day."

Studio? What studio? "Do you have the number?"

With more patience than Honey had ever known she had, she waited while the woman looked through some address book or other, then slowly recited the phone number. "I'm just his housekeeper, dear. I'm sure they'll be able to help you better than I could."

With a polite thank-you, Honey hung up, then began again, dialing the new number. Mr. Beau McGuire, she thought, had better have enough money to pay this phone bill!

"Good morning. National Studios," a light, sweet voice answered in sugary tones.

"Is Mr. McGuire there, please?" Honey asked.

"I'm sorry but he's filming right now. May I take a message?"

"Filming?" she repeated, knowing that she sounded as confused as she felt.

"Mr. McGuire is on the *Tomorrow's Promise* set, filming," the receptionist said, as if explaining things to a child.

Honey's mind started clicking. Beau McGuire. Of course! That Beau McGuire. He was the lead "hunk" in one of the most popular soap operas on TV. No wonder the receptionist thought she was an idiot. She had sounded more like a dumb fan than an otherwise intelligent woman trying to locate a missing father!

"May I speak to his secretary, please?"

After numerous clickings, Honey ended up with a woman who was whispering into the phone. Obviously filming was going on around her.

"How may I help you?" she asked softly, her tone nonetheless curt.

"Please tell Mr. McGuire that Honey Carter from Houston would like to speak with him regarding his daughter, Meagan."

"I can't. He's filming right now. Would you call back this afternoon? I'm sure he'll be available to speak to you then," the woman's whisper continued. She seemed to be in a hurry to hang up.

"Of course," Honey murmured, exasperation lacing her voice. "I wouldn't want to interfere with the great Mr. McGuire's work."

"Then I'll tell him to expect your call later, Miss uh . . ."

"Mrs. Carter." Honey bit out her name. "Thank you."

She placed the phone carefully back into its cradle, her eyes staring past the bright daffodil wallpaper, attempting to visualize the face of the man she had been trying to reach.

He was tall and broad shouldered, with the kind of build that always makes for popular male beefcake. He had dark hair, just the color of Meagan's, and the same penetrating holly-green eyes. The part he played on TV was very much the playboy, city-bred and city-born. He was probably very shallow. His sort had always turned her off.

"Well, Mr. McGuire," she said quietly, "let's hope we can keep our association as brief as possible . . . for both our sakes."

2

IMPATIENTLY, BEAU FLICKED BACK an errant raven-black lock of hair that kept falling onto his forehead as he stared in frustration at his temporary secretary. His movements were barely under control, his voice far darker and more demanding than usual. He tried to temper it, calling on all the self-possession he had in him.

"Okay, Joanne, please try to remember," he said, enunciating each word as if it would calm the panic building rapidly inside him. "What was her last name? Honey what? Did she say where she was? Was she in this city or state? Was she calling long-distance?"

Joanne wet her lips before answering, eyes darting toward the silent crew who had gathered around. "She said her name, but I don't remember it. I thought she was your daughter's nursery school teacher or something! I thought you'd know."

"Think, Joanne, think!" he urged. Logic, way in the back of his mind, told him her failure was all his fault. Joanne had replaced Toni, his flawless secretary of two years, only a week before. He could have told Toni anything, but Joanne was just filling in while Toni was taking her yearly vacation. He hadn't wanted to confide in Joanne about his private life. Too many temporaries were spies for the scandal sheets. "Was there static on the line? Could it have been out of state?"

Joanne nodded, relieved that she could give him some kind of useful information. "Yes, there was lots of static. I think she even mentioned that she was from somewhere, but I don't remember. You were busy and I had a long list of things to do, so I didn't pay a whole lot of attention to her because I thought you would know..." Her brow wrinkled in thought, then her eyes widened in surprise. "Her name was the same as one of the presidents'. Let's see—"

"Kennedy? Jefferson? Washington?" Beau interrupted, his impatience once more at the fore.

"Wait! You're making me lose my train of thought," she cried, as frustrated as he was. Then she smiled in victory. "Carter! That's it! Her name was Honey Carter!" She looked at him expectantly, but his features were just as troubled as before. Apparently the name meant nothing to him.

"Honey Carter," he repeated slowly, wondering if the name was supposed to ring a bell. He met so many people through his career, in restaurants, at parties. They all were convinced he would remember their names.

Len's loud sigh broke the mood. He turned and clapped his hands. "Okay, that's a wrap for today, folks." When the crew continued to stare at the scene in front of them, his bushy brows drew ominously together. "If you guys have nothing better to do, I'll see if I can find something for you." He looked at two of the younger men. "Bryan? Sam? Get moving!"

Beau was impervious to the noise around him. "She said she'd call back again this afternoon?" he asked.

Joanne nodded, her dark, well-shellacked hair bouncing as if it were a wig. "Oh, I remember something else. She said she was calling from Houston."

Beau let his pent-up breath escape. This woman who was supposed to keep up with his correspondence and monitor vital calls thought that Meagan had a nursery school teacher in Texas! "Thanks, Joanne."

She nodded, relief evident in her eyes.

"Need to use my office, Beau?" Len stood beside him, his forehead creased with worry lines much like the ones Beau had.

Beau smiled tightly. "Thanks. I do need to make a few phone calls."

His long stride ate up the distance as he left the studio and headed straight for Len's office. He rounded the massive, cluttered desk and reached for the telephone, dialing by memory the number he wanted. When the phone was answered, he uttered one name. "Lewell." After a minute or so, the man came on the line.

"This is McGuire. A Honey Carter from Houston, Texas, called me about Meagan. She's supposed to call back later this afternoon, and I want to know as much about her as you can find out before then."

Beau was silent a moment as the detective interrupted to bring him up to date. The man always spoke so loudly that Beau had to hold the phone away from his ear. But he heard every word. And the news was good.

"That's fine. So Honey Carter shouldn't be that hard to find."

When Lewell began to protest, Beau sighed. "Look, you've made a fortune off me, Lewell, and if I'm going to provide you with your own clues, then you can work overtime to get me the information I need." The phone crashed into its cradle more loudly than he intended, the sound reverberating throughout the room.

Len peeked cautiously around the doorway, a grin on his face. "Hey, don't break my phone. It's enough I have to work with guys like you. I don't need another handicap." He relaxed against the doorjamb, his long, thin arms crossed. "Do you want some privacy, or would you like to talk about it?" he asked.

"Come on in, Len," Beau said wearily.

After closing the door, Len moved to his desk, propping one hip on the edge. "Find out what you need to know?"

"Maybe," Beau said. "Something, at least."

"Hang in there. You'll find her."

Beau rubbed the back of his neck, willing himself to relax. He felt like a too tightly wound yo-yo about to spin off its string. "The longer Meagan's gone, the more I worry." He looked up at Len. "Once I get her back, I'll make damn sure this never happens again."

"How?"

"I don't know, yet. Maybe move. I just don't know."

"You could inform your secretary of minor events like this so she'd be better prepared," Len said dryly. "That might help."

"You're the one who hired a temporary, and she has to be prompted to remember a phone number?"

"She wasn't given a phone number. Remember?" Len sat down in his big desk chair, levering his spare frame into a more comfortable position.

"Right. But she should have thought to ask for one."

Len spread his hands in supplication. "Now wait a minute, Beau. You can't hold her responsible for what you didn't tell her. For all she knew, the call could have been a fan."

Beau sank into the deep-cushioned leather couch, leaning forward with his arms on his knees. For a minute he stared at his clasped hands, forcing the anger to dissipate so he could speak coherently. "The private investigator told me his man followed them to a small town called Tomball, in Texas. It's just outside of Houston. When the man spotted Pamela again this morning, he didn't see Meagan. It's possible Pamela dropped her off at this Honey Carter's house and that she has her now."

Len sat bolt upright. "Beau, are you sure?"

"Yes. The detective is getting me some more information on this Carter woman. He'll probably have something this evening. She'd better call back soon. The waiting is killing me."

"Don't worry. It will all work out," Len consoled. "You'll be finished filming tomorrow. The car accident the second unit is filming today will be good for the next few weeks. Tomorrow we'll shoot enough footage of you in the hospital, bandaged to the eyeballs and unable to speak to cover your absence."

When Beau looked up, his face was suddenly alight with the smile that had made him popular, a sex symbol to all the women who watched daytime TV. "Thanks, Len."

THE TELEVISION WARNED Honey of the impending storm. Hail, high winds, tornadoes and heavy rain were all forecast for later in the evening. Stalled in the Gulf for the past two days, the hurricane had made up its mind to touch land now at a spot just above Galveston Island. It was already brushing the coast with its advance squall line, which meant that it would come overland right into Houston.

Meagan was curled up next to Honey on the couch, her little head resting against the side of Honey's breast as she contentedly watched the trees outside the window bow and dance to the wind's orchestration.

Meagan hadn't seemed afraid of anything all day, except being more than a few feet away from Honey. Together, they had checked on the cattle, hens and cats, making sure there was enough feed for all of them in the barn. Wherever Honey went, Meagan dogged her tracks. Even to the bathroom. For a woman so committed to total privacy, who had cherished only her own company these past years, Honey hadn't had a single minute to herself. Oddly she hadn't minded at all. Her arm tightened ever so slightly, drawing Meagan even closer to her.

The little girl looked up, bright green eyes focusing on Honey's. "Mommy?" she asked in a tiny voice interwoven with fear.

"Mommy's not here, darling. But Honey is," she replied softly with a warm smile. "And soon your daddy will be here."

Meagan's eyes brightened, her instant grin dimpling her cheeks. "Is Daddy coming?" She skittered off the couch and ran across the room to stare out the window. "Daddy?"

"Soon, darling. Soon." Honey checked her watch. Maybe she had better try calling Beau McGuire now. If the storm arrived more quickly than the weatherman was predicting, the phone could soon be out of order.

One thing was certain: Meagan adored her father. Honey felt relieved to know she was doing the right thing. She had to wonder about a woman who would place a child in a van, though. Was the woman the mother or just a concerned citizen? No, she had to be the mother. So many questions kept disturbing Honey's peace of mind that she hadn't been able to work at all today. Thank goodness there was nothing pressing about the accounts she had to post.

She reached for the phone next to the couch and began dialing Beau McGuire's home number. Static crackled on the line. Maybe the elusive man would be in this time.

"Hello. This is Honey Carter. Is Mr. McGuire there?"

The voice reaching through the static sounded panicked. "Miss Carter? Where are you?" The voice was definitely a woman's, but she couldn't tell if it was the same one who had answered so sleepily that morning.

"I'm calling long-distance from Tomball, just outside Houston," she answered patiently. "Is Mr. McGuire there?"

"Not yet, but he said that if you called I was to get a number so he could reach you as soon as he came in," the woman said, obviously thrilled Honey had called. "Is Meagan with you?"

"Yes, and she's fine, but there's a hurricane brewing here, and I'm afraid the telephone lines might be down later." She gave the almost panicked woman her number and tried to reassure her once more that Meagan was quite happy for the time being. "But please tell Mr. McGuire that if he can't reach us, it's because of the storm. I didn't want him to worry about his daughter."

"Worry about Meagan? Are you kidding? That's all we've been able to think about!" Her voice faded, then Honey heard her say, "And whatever happens, don't let Pamela near her! Do you understand?"

Honey kept a tight rein on her anger. She wasn't sure what she was being accused of, but she didn't like the woman's tone one bit. "I don't know any Pamela."

"I'm sorry, but this has been a terrible strain on all of us. Just take good care of her until Beau can get there," the woman urged, her voice high-pitched and cracking through the receiver.

Honey hung up the phone. That woman acted as if she had volunteered for this job! She could have called the police and let them take care of the child instead of getting into what was rapidly becoming a mess with the father!

As if in response to Honey's agitation, Meagan climbed into her lap, throwing chubby little arms around Honey's neck and giving her a squeeze. "Mommy," she murmured against her neck, and Honey raised her arms to hold the sweet bundle closer.

Mentally she corrected Meagan's use of the term "Mommy," but her voice was still.

She tried to tell herself Meagan didn't know what the word meant, but she knew better. Meagan was a bright child, far brighter than the average three-year-old. Still she kept silent. Meagan's label warmed her insides like a good brandy. The feeling was too nice to deny.

She had thought she'd never hear that word spoken to her.

She gave Meagan a squeeze. "I'm Honey, sweetheart," she whispered. "Let's get your shoes, dumplin', and go to the grocery store. If this big storm really hits, the electricity will probably go off."

Meagan nodded solemnly, as if she understood all about hurricanes, then quickly ran up the stairs to the bedroom. Before Honey could reach for her car keys, Meagan was back, already plopped on the hall floor, attempting to studiously place the left sandal on her pudgy right foot. Trying to hold in her chuckle, Honey kneeled to help her.

The store was crowded with other families heeding the storm watch. Honey hefted Meagan into the basket seat and wheeled down the aisles, feeling a curious contentment at joining the ranks of other mothers doing the same. As hard as she tried not to attach herself to Meagan, the child seemed to be filling a void in Honey that she hadn't even been aware of. She shook her head as if to banish the thought. She wouldn't think about that. Not today.

Candles, Sterno, extra canned foods began to fill their basket. After glancing at a few of the other shoppers' carts, Honey realized canned food wasn't enough. She also needed powdered milk, fresh fruit, cheeses and cookies. Her last purchase brought a sweet smile to Meagan's face, but she uttered no sound or squeals of delight like the other children . . . until they reached the children's book section. At Meagan's insistence, Honey wound up buying six.

"Do you like this kind of book, Meagan?" she asked as she picked up a few other goodies, and the child nodded, her large green eyes wide.

"Aunt Shelly buys those for me," she said with a dimpled smile.

Well, at least Meagan was pleased.

The phone was ringing as they entered the house. Honey had Meagan perched on one hip, a bag of groceries on the other. She fumbled for the light switch with her elbow. Even though it was only six o'clock, it was dark as midnight outside.

"Carter residence," she answered breathlessly, only to hear the other end of the line click. The connection was broken. Shrugging, she put Meagan and the grocery bag down and began to unload the van. According to the radio, the storm was due to hit Houston in the morning, so she and Meagan would have a hot dinner, a warm bath and an early bedtime.

Her thoughts paused briefly on Meagan's father. Because of the storm, he might not be able to come for his daughter for several days.

"SHELLY, CAN YOU BOOK a flight to Houston for me? The sooner the better!" Beau hollered over his shoulder as he walked in the front door of the apartment, throwing his topcoat on the couch and heading straight into his bedroom.

Shelly rose from her curled up position in the chair, the textbook she'd been studying sliding to the floor. "Did you get hold of that Honey Carter woman?" she called to his retreating back.

When his mumbling was all she heard in reply, Shelly went to the door of his room and looked in. Beau was quickly stuffing his overnight bag with a handful of clean clothes. "I gave you her number. Did you call?" she asked again.

"I tried. Either there was no answer or I couldn't get through because there's a hurricane brewing down there. They've got a tornado alert on, too. I have to get Meagan out of there!"

"Calm down, Beau." Shelly stepped into the room, crossing her arms and scowling at her big brother. "Whoever the woman is who has Meagan, she's no villain. I spoke to her, remember? After all, she notified you of Meagan's whereabouts and seemed concerned that you know Meagan was all right."

Beau could tell from the look in Shelly's eyes that she was just as worried about him as she was about Meagan.

Nevertheless, he was unable to hide his expression. "Meagan belongs home with us, not in the middle of a dangerous storm." He dropped a few extra shirts into his suitcase and stood up, the intense pain in his green eyes shattering her composure. "Can you please call for me, Shel? Any flight will do."

"Right away," she said, going quickly to the phone on his nightstand. She flipped through the phone book until she found the number she wanted, then began dialing.

Beau's thoughts flew to his daughter, so tiny, so precious, so delightfully a child. Could Pamela and her crazy boyfriend have scarred Meagan in some way? He prayed not. Whatever had happened, his daughter had to be safe and secure. He forced himself to hang on to that thought.

He snapped the suitcase shut and swung it off the bed. Meagan was part of him. He had seen her through first feedings, diapers, teething, even chicken pox.

And he knew how she hated thunderstorms.

She would wake up and fly to him for protection. Then she'd cuddle into his arms as he crooned silly nonsense tunes, relaxing her enough to fall back to sleep because she believed her daddy was a giant who could protect her from everything. And now she was in the hands of some stranger. . . .

Shelly's voice broke into his thoughts. "Beau, I can't get you into Houston. All flights are canceled until further notice. The best you can do is go to the airport and wait until it's clear, then get on the first available flight."

He frowned. "What about nearby cities? I'll rent a car and drive the rest of the way."

"Tonight?"

"I have to go to Meagan."

Shelly dialed again as he stowed his shaving gear in the side pocket of his overnight bag. When she looked up a moment later, her face was as drawn as his. "You're going to Austin, but that's two hundred miles away!"

"Which means the airport there will still be open."

"But that's such a long drive heading into a storm, Beau."

"I have no alternative," he said quietly.

"Right." She began talking into the phone once more.

He passed through the living room into Meagan's room. A few minutes later he had grabbed up a handful of little girl's clothing and her well-loved but weather-beaten rag doll.

Beau stuffed Meagan's clothes into the side of the case, his mind racing with the things he had to do. Thank God he could count on Shelly to hold the fort until he got back. She was as capable a secretary as she was a teacher.

He heard Shelly's voice dwindle away, and the phone hit the cradle. Leaning down, he zipped his small case closed, then accepted the piece of paper she was holding out to him.

"Beau, please be careful. If anything happened to you—" Her voice broke suddenly, and Beau looked up, seeing the not quite formed tears in her usually mischievous eyes.

He muttered an expletive under his breath, taking her in his arms. "Hey, nothing's going to happen to me, Shel. I'm just going to pick up Meagan and come back. That's all."

"I'm worried. That storm . . ." Her voice was muffled against the softness of his sweater.

"That storm will pass and then we'll be back. Just give me a few days and we'll all be where we should be—together again. For good this time," he promised, as if it were already carved in stone. He said it just as much to reassure himself as to calm her.

"WELL, MEAGAN, what shall we do?" Honey led the way out of the kitchen, carefully holding a tray with two mugs of cold chocolate milk and several chocolate chip cookies. She knew that Meagan was right behind her, following her footsteps, and somehow she felt comforted by that.

"Daddy?" Meagan asked, clutching her gray one-eared bunny as she almost tripped on her nightgown. "Is Daddy coming?"

"Soon, darling," Honey said, setting the tray on an end table before turning to snuggle Meagan into the corner of the couch.

"Okay," Meagan said, trying to pick the remaining eye out of her bunny's less than round head. Suddenly her bright green eyes lit up, and her curls bounced as she raised her head. "Swing?" she asked hopefully.

"Sewing?" Honey repeated with a slight frown, wondering how a child knew about such things.

Meagan nodded her head. "Swing," she repeated.

"Okay, sweetie. Tomorrow." Honey's mind was in a whirl. What did three-year-olds know about sewing? Could they even hold a needle without pricking themselves? Honey wasn't even sure if *she* could wield a needle!

Earlier that afternoon Honey and Meagan had watched the soap opera Beau McGuire starred in. Meagan had become excited, calling "Daddy!" every time he had appeared on the screen.

Honey had ignored his good looks and his superior acting skills. Those weren't requirements for taking care of his child. But secretly she had hoped he would send someone else to pick up Meagan. He was too attractive and too intimidating on TV for her to deal with. If he was that potent on the tube, what would he possibly be like in person? She'd had enough experience with handsome men to last her a lifetime.

She and Meagan curled under the large crocheted afghan on the couch while Honey read from one of the books they had bought earlier. Meagan studied every picture, then carefully explained it to Honey, right down to letters and numbers. The child had obviously been well taught to have such an extensive knowledge at such a tender age, Honey thought. Her heart was bursting with an almost maternal tenderness that had been foreign to her until now. The feeling was new but very nice.

If things had only turned out differently, she might have had a child Meagan's age.

Just then, the lights flickered and a loud clap of thunder rumbled through the room. Meagan's pudgy little arms jerked in reaction to the sound, her mug of chocolate milk splashing Honey's robe as the small child began to cry. She crowded into Honey's lap like a dog burrowing for a bone.

"Wha . . . !" Honey exclaimed.

Suddenly Meagan sat up, cringing as she saw Honey's robe. "I sorry! I sorry!" she cried, her appeal striking an instant chord in Honey's heart.

"Hey, hey, it's all right, darling," Honey crooned, gathering her back into her arms. "It's okay," she soothed, realizing somehow that Meagan was more afraid of her reaction to the spilled chocolate milk than she was of the heart-stopping thunder outside.

Why was she so upset over a little accident? Could someone have punished her in the past for doing what was probably natural to any three-year-old? Honey's hands trembled with the thought.

Again the lights blinked, and seconds later a gust of wind shuddered against the windows, making them rattle ominously in response. The storm had arrived.

Meagan snuggled against Honey, and she wrapped both arms around the child, holding her close in comfort as her hands absently stroked the child's shoulders. Her eyes were glued to the ten o'clock news as the announcer warned that the hurricane was already moving inland from the Galveston coast. The electricity wouldn't be on for long if that was the case, which meant they ought to go to bed soon.

Meagan was nearly asleep before Honey checked the flashlights for batteries, wrapped the refrigerator and freezer in quilts to help keep the cold in and switched lights off. She put the little girl in the center of the bed, watching her cozily curl into a tight ball. Once Meagan had been reassured, it didn't take any time at all for her to fall sound asleep.

Honey lay down herself, closed her eyes and ignored the storm that had begun to batter the walls of her sturdy house. It had stood this long; it would surely withstand another bout with the fickle Houston climate. Sighing, Honey snuggled up and fitted herself spoon fashion against the little girl's back. She refused to think how easily she had become attached to Meagan. If she did, then she would be forced to admit her own loneliness. She could always do that later, after Meagan's father came and took his daughter away, and Honey was alone once more.

BEAU SLOWED THE RENTAL CAR to a crawl as he rechecked the directions to Honey Carter's house by the interior light. Lewell had had no problem locating her or forwarding the information. He peered through the rain-streaked windshield, squinting past a heavy veil of water. The detective might have said she was in Houston, but it was definitely the outskirts of the city—the distant outskirts. It looked every bit like empty countryside to him. There was a house every couple hundred yards, the road he was on was graveled instead of paved and the trees—a mixture of majestic oaks and sky-stroking pines—were huge.

Rain battered the windshield, almost blinding him. If it hadn't been for the occasional light by the side of the road proclaiming another property entrance, he wouldn't have been able to find his way at all. At least the lights defined the right side of the road. The left side he could only wonder about. Fourth. Fifth. Sixth. There it was, the entrance leading to the seventh house on the right. Carefully he turned in, praying to avoid the deep, already overflowing ditches on either side of the drive.

His hands were welded to the steering wheel as he maneuvered up the curving driveway. Where in hell was the house? He squinted again, trying to see through the dark and the wind-driven rain to where he was going. There was nothing ahead but blackness until a jagged streak of lightning arced across the sky, illuminating a white brick house with a soaring two-story facade almost directly in front of him.

Thank goodness! He didn't think he could have driven another mile, no matter how much Meagan needed him. He killed the engine and wiped the beaded perspiration from his forehead, clenching and unclenching his hands to ease the stiffness. Thunder again rumbled through the night. He checked his watch by the light from the panel. Two o'clock. He'd have to wake them, though he doubted Meagan would be sleeping through a storm like this.

His overtired imagination could almost hear her crying out his name, and as if running to answer her call, he jumped from the car and sprinted toward the overhang partially protecting the doorway from the downpour.

AT FIRST, THE BANGING SEEMED to be taking place in her dream, but when the staccato beat continued, it finally intruded on Honey's unconsciousness enough to draw her out of the cozy nest of sleep. With her eyes closed, she listened, barely able to drag herself from the comfort of sleep to pay attention to the storm outside. But when dim shouts of "Hello" finally drifted up to her, she was instantly awake.

With a quick glance at a sleeping Meagan, Honey slipped from the covers and padded toward the closed bedroom door, the big flashlight from her bedside table in her hand. Her tailored cream-and-brown pajamas were protection enough for her not to bother with a robe. She pattered down the steps barefoot as quickly as she could, listening with one ear to some man shouting on her doorstep while she monitored the weather with the other. It didn't sound as if the hurricane had hit full force yet. But she was sure it was close.

What kind of idiot would be out on a night like this? An escapee from a mental institution? A criminal? A tourist passing through? It certainly wouldn't be one of her neighbors; they were smart enough to stay in on a night like this.

By the time she got to the front door, the shouting was even louder. Clearly her visitor wasn't anyone she knew. Locals had better manners than to bellow into the night.

She tried the hall light, glad to see the electricity was still on. "Hold on! I'm coming!" she called, struggling impatiently with the door lock. Too bad her rifle was behind the seat of the old pickup she drove around the property. Everyone in these rural areas kept one to kill rattlers or relieve injured animals. But the heavy six-cell flashlight would have to do. If she bopped someone over the head with it, he'd drop with a thud.

As she carefully opened the door in the middle of a frantic knock, a fierce gust of wet wind literally propelled the man inside, forcing Honey back into the hallway, barely able to maintain her balance.

Still clutching the flashlight, she held it ready, waiting to see whether he was friend or foe. Surprisingly she was calm.

But the second she saw his face, she knew who he was. Beau McGuire. That cap of black curly hair and the bright green eyes squinting blindly back at her confirmed any doubts she might have had. His broad shoulders almost filled the doorway. He turned and shut the door, holding his body against it to latch it securely.

"Mr. McGuire?" she asked breathlessly. They were both rigid, as if frozen in time as each waited for some reaction from the other. He turned around to face her fully, and now that the door was closed there was no sound in the entryway except for his heavy breathing.

He stood still, narrowing his eyes, then shielding them with his hand from the bright hallway light until they could adjust.

"Yes. Mrs. Carter?"

"Yes," she said, breathing more easily now.

"I'm sorry to barge in like this, but I know how Meagan is during storms, so I came as quickly as I could."

She nodded. "Well, Meagan's sound asleep. She seems to have forgotten there's a storm going on." Curious, she studied him. "It's the middle of the night. Did you drive through that mess?"

"I'm afraid so," he replied. Now that his eyes had adjusted to the light, his hand dropped from his brow. He could see her features as clearly as she could see his. Her honey-blond hair was curled and flowing around her head like a halo, and her bright, wide, brown eyes stared at him as if mesmerized, her full lips parted slightly. She looked as if she had just been made wild, wonderful love to and was reveling in the afterglow.

Her next words came out in a rush. "Well, you shouldn't have. It's dangerous driving in this, to say nothing of exhausting. You should have waited until morning when you could at least see through the rain."

He shook his head. "I couldn't wait. The Houston airport is closed, and they told me that Austin might have to close, too, if the hurricane moves inland as it's supposed to."

"Then how on earth did you get here?"

"I flew into Austin while I still could, then rented a car and drove here."

"Good grief. That's almost two hundred miles." She could see the lines of fatigue that etched his features, and the slumping shoulders. He was almost asleep on his feet.

"I was worried about Meagan," he said, his tone of voice underlining his tiredness.

She reached for the old-fashioned newel post to steady herself, and nodded. "Let me show you that she's perfectly all right, then perhaps we can all get some sleep." She kept her voice deliberately light, but the airy quality was really due to lack of oxygen. Beau McGuire was having a very strange effect on her.

"Good thing the electricity is still on," she murmured. She studied him as thoroughly as he was staring at her. A tight, drawn look creased the corners of his mouth. "You're soaking wet, too," she declared.

"It's raining pretty hard," was his answer as he took in her well-scrubbed face, devoid of any makeup. He noticed her cream-and-brown pajamas. There was no frilly, feminine robe like most women he knew usually wore. In fact, no one he knew in New York even owned a pair of serviceable pajamas like those, nor did they ever go to bed with such well-scrubbed faces. At least not his bed.

She could almost read his thoughts. Honey straightened. "Are you hungry? Do you want something hot or maybe a shot of whiskey?" she asked matter-of-factly, taking in his soaked topsiders, tan cords and the now rumpled pullover with a drop of mustard on the front. The small animal insignia on his sweater, along with the rest of his clothing, proclaimed him a preppy.

That definition almost made her smile as she took another look at him. Out here on the outskirts of Houston, where everybody had some acreage, no one dressed without a pair of jeans as well as a hat to keep the sun or rain off. And here Meagan's father stood before her, a preppy. The grin finally won out.

Beau was wiping his damp hands on his trousers and looked up just in time to see a tiny dimple appear. Somehow it didn't match her serviceable pajamas. "After I see that Meagan's all right, I'd love some whiskey," he said quietly. "I managed to grab a couple of hot dogs just outside Austin." Every muscle in his body ached from the strain of driving through the storm for the past three hours. He was too damn tired to think straight.

Without another word, she padded toward what he assumed was the living room, flipped on a wall switch and headed toward a large barrel bar standing in the corner. Two swivel chairs stood in front of it, and he followed her, stopping to lean on one. "I'd like to see Meagan first."

"Might as well take this with you," she said calmly, reaching for a highball glass and filling it halfway with Kentucky's best. She poured with a steady hand, giving him almost exactly a double shot. She poured another, smaller one for herself. She held his glass out, careful not to touch his fingers when he grasped it. "Cheers," she said, and took a sip from her glass.

His eyes narrowed in puzzlement. She looked feminine enough, he thought. Full, pert breasts, a neat set of hips, a nice walk that imitated a skater's glide even in bare feet. Rare.

And a whiskey drinker.

"Follow me," she said, leading the way back to the entry hall and the stairs.

Downing his drink in three quick gulps, he set his glass down with a thump. Whiskey warmth began to radiate through his body, instantly warding off the damp chill of the storm. By the time he reached the landing, he was beginning to feel halfway human again.

"First, I'll show you Meagan, then the guest bedroom, Mr. McGuire. Perhaps we'll all get some sleep yet." An extra hard gust hit the windows, rattling them noisily, and the lights flickered.

"And not a moment too soon," he said under his breath, wondering how he had had the nerve to drive through such weather.

Honey turned to the right, leading him to her bedroom. Opening the door, she pressed a finger against her lips and shone her flashlight on the wall so its beam was reflected around them. He nodded to show he understood.

They tiptoed in, Beau's eyes adjusting to the darkness until he could make out the little bundle huddled in the center of the big bed, her tousled black curls framing the face he loved so much. He moved to the bedside, bending down as Honey focused the light toward Meagan's feet so he could see her better.

She watched silently. Whatever she had expected, it wasn't the utter tenderness of Beau McGuire's expression. His whole face seemed to alter from highly reserved and exhausted to the total and absolute devotion of a father for his daughter. It was something she had never seen before in a man. In slow motion he lowered his head and kissed Meagan's cheek, feather-light so she wouldn't be disturbed.

Even so, Meagan smiled sweetly at his touch, hugging her one-eared rabbit closer to her, but giving no signs of waking.

With equal stealth, he moved back to the door and stood there, staring down at Honey. "Thank you," he said in a voice gravelly with emotion. "For everything."

"You're welcome," she whispered. Turning quickly, she led him to the door across the hall. "Here's your room. There are clean sheets on the bed because I was going to put Meagan in here, but she seemed so content . . ." Honey's voice trailed off.

Beau nodded, giving her a quick smile. "I understand. We'll talk in the morning, Mrs. Carter," he said in a low voice. "Please let Meagan know I'm here as soon as she wakes up."

She smiled, that lone dimple surprising him again. "I will. Now get some sleep. You look bushed." Her words were matter-of-fact, but her tone revealed her genuine concern.

This time he gave her his patented heart-melting grin. "Good night."

worlds or just a job, but he knew he avoided her
genuine warmth.

This simple gaze had his emotion free-wheeling.

She knew what...

_____ **3** _____

IN LESS THAN A MINUTE Beau stripped off his soggy
clothes and climbed between the coolness of the fresh
sheets. Because he felt so wiped out emotionally and
physically, he thought he'd have no trouble falling
right into a deep sleep. But he did.

The storm buffeted the upstairs windows, and he
could hear the sounds Mrs. Carter made as she went
down the stairs. He knew she was checking the doors,
turning out the lights, securing the house again.

Her last words, "You look bushed," echoed through
his mind, and he grinned. No mothering, no sweet
talk, just a simple statement.

He frowned. He'd forgotten to ask Lewell if she was
married, divorced or widowed. He assumed she was
married, because she called herself Mrs., but her bed
was obviously empty of a man. Perhaps he was on a
trip somewhere. It was the only explanation his tired
mind could come up with. How else could she keep
up this property? Even in the rain, he realized the
houses were set far apart on lots of three or four acres.

He sighed and stretched. Right now he'd give a
week's wages to be comforted against a woman's

breast so he could fall asleep. But not this woman. She was too much like a man for his taste—a whiskey-sipping, none-too-sympathetic woman. A vision of her lush figure appeared, but he pushed it away. It took more than a figure to make a woman; it took warmth, softness and a beguiling manner....

Then he remembered the dimple in her cheek and wondered at how he had longed to touch it. At that thought, he grinned again. Every woman he had chosen to spend time with, both before and after Pamela, had been ultrafeminine. Yet those same women never hesitated to cheat on him or any other guy if they were so inclined. So far his current taste in women left a lot to be desired. But it didn't really matter, because he had Shelly and Meagan. The other females in his life weren't prospective brides; they were only momentary companions.

The door across the hall clicked softly closed, telling him that the house was now secure and everyone was tucked in for the night. The whistling wind and pounding rain finally lulled Beau to sleep.

THOUGH IT WAS still dark and gloomy, with heavy rain assaulting the house and grounds, Meagan was awake a little after seven. Ignoring her at first, Honey curled deeper into the covers, reluctant to face the day.

"Mommy?" Meagan attempted to whisper in her ear, but it sounded more like a shout.

Honey's hand emerged from the bedclothes, awkwardly patting the little girl's head. "Go back to sleep, sweetheart. It's too early to be up," she mumbled, hoping her advice would be heeded. She should have known better.

Meagan bounced on the bed, giggling at Honey's closed eyes, which she tried to open with tiny nimble fingers. When that didn't work, she stuck a small finger in Honey's mouth. "Talk, Mommy," she ordered, and Honey couldn't help but grin. She grappled with Meagan, and they began rolling about the bed, giggles and laughter momentarily holding at bay the roar of the storm.

Then she remembered Beau McGuire was across the hall. There was no sense telling Meagan about her father now. He was exhausted and needed all the sleep he could get in the next few hours.

"Shhh," she said, touching a finger to her mouth. "Let's go downstairs and see if we can get some breakfast. We have company in the other bedroom, and we don't want to wake him up. Okay?" she whispered.

Meagan's dark curls bobbed up and down, suddenly serious with the task ahead. "Shh. No wake up," she repeated.

"Right." They made a game of tiptoeing across the carpet, opening the door and making their way stealthily down the stairs. Only the tiniest of giggles gave away their presence.

Honey reached the landing, and her heart gave a gentle squeeze as she watched Meagan earnestly trying to follow her steps. Tiptoeing and teetering, the little girl finally reached the bottom. She was such a dear little sweetheart.

Honey turned on the portable transistor radio on the counter, but nothing happened. Sometime during the night the electricity had gone out. Flipping a switch, she changed it to battery-operated so she could listen to the weather report. A monotone announcer's voice told of the hurricane now situated just inland from Galveston and already raising the water level of the bay by nine feet. There were fallen trees everywhere, and no one was supposed to travel, even in an emergency. Later that morning, the winds would be gusting over a hundred miles an hour. Honey could only pray that the creek at the back of her property wouldn't flood so far it would reach the barn. The stream was probably full enough right now to flood the access roads leading to the main highway.

As the announcer's voice droned on, she stared out the window, verifying that the storm in front of the hurricane had intensified in both rain and wind. According to the radio, the eye of the hurricane had just reached Houston.

Last night she had filled several gallon containers with water and had lined them up against the kitchen wall. She had also filled the sink, and there were buckets in the bathroom for washing and flushing.

She could always borrow her neighbor Mac's generator if she needed electricity in an emergency. There were two stoves in the kitchen—her electric range and an old wood-burning stove that had been there ever since the house was built—so she'd have no problem with cooking. She lit some kindling inside the black iron door, making sure it caught before closing it and a few of the vents.

"Want some cereal?" Honey asked, and the child nodded from her perch on the counter. Her thumb was thrust in her mouth, her wide green eyes observing every move Honey made. "And some cocoa?" Meagan nodded again, her curls bobbing adorably.

Within minutes breakfast was ready. Honey swept Meagan off the counter and seated her at the butcher-block table. She placed the cocoa in front of Meagan along with a bowl of cereal the little girl had chosen yesterday at the grocery store.

Neither of them heard the footsteps on the stairs, but when Honey looked up Beau was in the kitchen doorway, one hand braced against the jamb. His tan cords were slung low on his hips. His hair was mussed, his feet bare on the green-and-yellow tile floor. A button-down shirt covered his arms and shoulders, but only a single button fastened near his waist kept it from baring his chest. He looked masculine in every way.

His green eyes were on his daughter. Honey stared at him as he watched Meagan, love and some kind of pain beaming from his eyes. Her heart went out to him, certain now that she had done the right thing by calling him instead of the police.

"Meagan," he said softly. She looked up and her eyes grew even wider, her mouth forming a small round O. With lightning speed, she erupted from the chair and hurled herself into her father's arms as he bent down, hugging him tightly around his neck as she made the soft cooing sounds that only a child can produce.

It was Honey's turn to swallow the lump in her throat.

Beau closed his eyes as he hugged his daughter fiercely. When Meagan leaned back, placing her plump hands on either side of his face, his smile was brilliant, almost a match for Meagan's.

Meagan brushed her fingertips along her father's unshaven jaw. "Daddy!" she giggled delightfully. "You're furry!" It broke the ice for all of them.

Beau managed a wobbly chuckle. "I wanted to see you, make sure you were all right before I shaved," he said softly.

"Daddy?" Her eyes were still alight with the wonder of seeing him. "Meagan want to watch you shave."

"Yes, sweetheart," he said as he gently released her. He stood erect, running a hand over his beard. "As soon as I get the rest of my gear out of the car."

Honey turned toward the stove, ready to pop some bread into the oven. She was hungry now. "There's an umbrella in the hall closet," she said. "There are also several pairs of black rubber boots. But check them for size."

"Thank you," he said. "Are they your husband's?"

"Mr. Carter died." The void in her voice told him of her loss better than a thousand words could.

"I'm sorry." He hesitated. He wasn't sure what else to say.

"It's all right." She continued to occupy herself at the stove.

"Do you live here alone?" His hand was buried in Meagan's curls as she wrapped herself around his leg while watching Honey making toast. He still felt a bit groggy.

After a pause, she turned toward him, her brown eyes lowered. "Yes. My husband died three years ago."

Sensing she was reluctant to discuss it further, Beau sought a change in topic. "We never did get a chance to talk about Meagan last night. Where on earth did you find her? How did you manage to contact me?"

Honey combed her fingers through her hair, brushing it out of the way and back over her shoulder. "I found Meagan in the back of my van around three a.m. Monday morning. She had a small case with her things in it. Attached was a note with your name and number on it. At four a.m. I tried to call you, but I reached a very sleepy lady instead." She raised her brows in silent query, but he merely nodded for her to go on. "Then I called the studio, and your secretary gave me the brush-off, telling me you were busy at the moment. You obviously know the rest or you wouldn't be here."

"Where's Aunt Shelly?" Meagan asked as she went back to the table, scooting her little bottom into the center of the chair to begin eating again.

Honey wondered whether Meagan used "aunt" in the sense of a relative or as a nickname for some good friend. He seemed the sort of man who would have lots of women around. His profession alone would insure that.

Beau must have read her mind. "Shelly is my sister. She lives with me and helps take care of Meagan."

"I see." Honey plucked the toast from the oven and began buttering it. When she sprinkled some sugar and cinnamon over it and put it on the table next to Meagan's bowl, Beau peered over, his dark green eyes taking in the cereal and Meagan's toast and cocoa.

His loving arm moved the toast out of Meagan's reach. "That's far too much sugar for a little girl," he said, softly but firmly.

"What are you talking about?" Honey asked, confused.

"Sugar in her cocoa if you used the brand on the counter, sugar on her toast, and there's more sugar in that brand of cereal than in any other."

"Good grief, I didn't even think," she began, realizing just how much sugar she *had* given the child.

"I know. It took me a while to catch on, too," he said, chuckling softly. "Too bad children don't come with their own manuals on how to raise them."

"I'm sorry," Honey said, scooping the toast off the table completely. "You hear about sugar all the time, but I've never... I don't have many opportunities to entertain children, so I never thought about it." She wasn't about to admit how little she knew about children. Weren't all women supposed to be born with that knowledge?

"Is there a dentist lurking in your family tree?" he teased, green eyes sparkling mischievously. Meagan's bright gaze darted from one to the other as it did when she watched cartoons on TV.

"Of course," she retorted dryly. "But since I was only caring for Meagan temporarily, I had to work fast."

A loud roll of thunder shook the house. Meagan's lower lip quivered, and she quickly sped around the table and crawled into her father's lap.

A lump formed in Honey's throat as she watched Meagan reach for her daddy's neck and cling, her face buried against his neck.

"You didn't bring your wife with you, Mr. McGuire?" she asked.

"Please call me Beau," he said. "And I don't have a wife. Meagan's mother—" he looked down at the top of his daughter's curly head as it burrowed deeper against his chest "—decided to take Meagan on an adventure. It ended in your van."

"I see," she said soberly, able to read his expression well enough to know he didn't want to discuss the matter in front of his daughter. Meagan peeked up at her, and Honey couldn't help smiling back.

"How long do you think this storm will last?" Beau asked, changing the subject abruptly.

"It could be three or four days before it runs its course. Meanwhile there's bound to be a lot of flooding, washed-out roads, downed power lines."

He frowned. "That long?"

"I'm afraid so. It's a major hurricane. We're lucky we're at the farthest point from the storm right now. It loses strength as it moves inland." She felt almost apologetic. Now that he had Meagan, she knew he wanted to return home right away.

Then he grinned, and it almost took her breath away. "I'm no expert on hurricanes. I just hear about them on the news, and they're usually pretty far removed from my world."

Just then, the whole house shook from thunder that was so close it seemed almost directly overhead.

"This one's definitely making its presence known," Honey remarked as Meagan began to wail in obvious fear of the storm. Honey pivoted quickly and walked out the kitchen door. "If you'd like something to eat, Beau, please help yourself. I've got to get dressed and do chores," she said over her shoulder.

In less than fifteen minutes, she had washed up and slipped into a pair of jeans and a Western-cut shirt.

She ran over a mental list of things to do. Between the wood stove in the kitchen and the fireplace in the living room, the house should stay warm and dry. She'd have to check on the supply of wood, however, and carry some in from the barn if necessary.

Today, instead of her usual hand-tooled boots, she wore running shoes. Except for tramping out to the barn, she wouldn't be going far.

In no time she was ready, her hair brushed back in a loose topknot. They were sure to be locked in here together for at least the next several days. She stared at herself in the mirror, wondering how she was going to keep Beau entertained for that length of time and still stay far enough away not to be swayed by his very male magnetism. They were clearly from two different worlds, but she didn't need any schoolgirl crushes at her age. "Just stay cool, Honey," she warned her reflection. "The city boy will be gone soon."

When she got downstairs, she could hear Meagan chattering away to her father, using words she didn't even know that child understood. She halted a foot away from the kitchen doorway, eavesdropping on their conversation. It wasn't until her father failed to answer one of Meagan's questions that the little girl looked up and saw Honey hovering in the doorway.

Without a word, Meagan jumped off the chair and ran to Honey, hugging her legs just like she had Beau's earlier. Honey smiled and gently patted her on the head.

Beau's eyes locked with hers, and she felt a flash of jealousy from him, along with something else she couldn't define. A sadness perhaps? She wasn't sure.

"Meagan feed the chickens?" the little girl mumbled against Honey's leg before raising her small heart-shaped face, an impish glint in her eyes.

Honey grinned, unable to keep her response from shining right back. "Not today, moppet. Why don't you go get dressed instead?"

"And finish your breakfast," Beau said as he turned back to the stove and spooned eggs onto a platter. Obviously he wasn't a cereal eater.

He sniffed the eggs, then looked at her. "These eggs were in the refrigerator so I used them, but I'm not sure they're fresh. They were larger than usual and have dark yolks."

She picked up the child and walked on into the room, carrying Meagan to her chair and sitting her at the table. "Those're guinea hen eggs. They're perfectly fine to eat, just a little different."

"Guinea hens? Aren't all hens the same?"

"No. There must be five dozen varieties, just like cattle. Guinea hens look like a cross between a turkey and a pheasant, and they're even dumber, but they keep the crickets, grasshoppers and other bugs under control."

He checked the eggs again, cautiously. "Are you—"

"Sure?" she said, smiling. "Yes."

"Meagan's going to eat some," he warned.

"And if there are any left, I will, too." Her breezy answer must have allayed his fears, because he finally sat down at the table and began to test his own cooking.

She poured half a cup of coffee for herself, watching him through her lashes. Beau McGuire was one very handsome man with as much sex appeal as any two men had a right to. Her husband, Peter, had been sexy. . . .

It took Meagan two seconds to jump from the table and dash down the hallway, taking the stairs a careful step at a time. Beau listened, a frown etching his brow.

"She could fall," he worried aloud. "She's not used to stairs."

"She's getting used to them. Isn't that important?" Honey had never thought of a child having to get used to steps. She had just taken it for granted that Meagan could manage them. It was her turn to frown.

He smiled at her ruefully. "Sorry if I sound like a mother hen," he said. "I guess I'm still upset over this whole episode." He sighed. "I've raised Meagan since birth. Her mother never wanted her. But last week

Pamela kidnapped her and held Meagan for ransom. Then she panicked and took off across the country. I've had private detectives following them ever since they left New York, but it wasn't until yesterday that I really had any hope of getting her back."

"My God," Honey whispered, unable to understand a mother doing that to her own child. "You mean . . ." She stopped to clear her throat, then began again. "Are you saying that Meagan's mother kidnapped her for money? All the way from New York? And that her mother *never* wanted her? Ever?"

Beau nodded grimly, pushing away his plate of eggs. "That's about it."

"That's just awful," Honey murmured, trying to absorb it all and yet not quite able to.

The kitchen was so quiet they could hear Meagan running out of the bedroom and down the hall to the stairs. Then the sound changed to *thump-dump*, as she hopped down each of the steps two feet at a time.

Honey looked at Beau, her face still somber from their discussion. "The storm is going to get worse before it gets better. Please make yourself at home."

"Thanks." Beau stood and scraped his eggs into the sink, his appetite apparently gone. "I don't think I could drive in this weather if my life depended on it. Not after last night. I'm not even sure how I made it here."

"I don't have a disposal," she interjected.

"What?" He looked confused.

She smiled. "I don't have a garbage disposal. I put all the scraps in that covered bowl there." She pointed to a yellow bowl with a white plastic lid in the corner of the counter. "Then I feed it to the animals," she explained patiently, remembering he was in unfamiliar territory.

Beau smiled in apology. "Er, sorry about that."

She went to the sink, and with an economy of motion she scooped up the eggs and put them in the bowl. She secured the lid, turning around just in time to see Meagan seated on the hall floor, buckling her sandals, carefully putting the left one on the right foot and vice versa.

Meagan was so proud of her accomplishment that neither of them had the heart to tell her she had put them on the wrong feet. Again Beau and Honey exchanged an understanding smile as they both noticed at the same time that she had also put on her shirt inside out and backward.

Meagan grinned at Honey. "See, Mommy? I dress myself," she announced, smoothing the shirt over her fat little tummy.

"I see you did, darlin'." Honey's voice was a gentle caress, her pride evident.

Beau frowned, his hands tucked in his back pockets as he watched the two of them. "Mommy?" he said, raising an eyebrow at Honey.

"No matter how many times I correct her, she seems to say it anyway," Honey defended, putting the salt and pepper shakers back on the spice shelf.

"Meagan," Beau began, hunkering down in front of her. "Mrs. Carter isn't your mommy. She's just a good friend. You should call her..." He glanced up, and she nodded. "You should call her Honey."

Meagan's bottom lip trembled. "But I want her to be my mommy."

"But I..." Beau began, only this time Meagan turned wide green eyes up at Honey.

"Don't you love me?" she asked Honey with child-like simplicity.

"Of course I do!" Honey said, kneeling beside Beau and in front of Meagan. "It's just that Mommy is the name you usually use when..." It was her turn to hesitate. She glanced at Beau, who was still frowning, and then back again at Meagan. "I'll tell you what," Honey said. "You can call me Mommy until you leave here, okay?"

Meagan cheered up instantly. "Okay," she said, nodding vigorously.

Relieved, Honey got to her feet and went to put on the long raincoat she kept on a peg just inside the back door.

"You're not going outside, are you?" Beau asked incredulously.

"I'm going thirty feet away from the house to the barn. Hurricane or no, I have to feed the cats and chickens," she pointed out.

"But this is a hurricane!"

"The animals have to eat."

His jaw hardened. "You should stay inside where it's safe."

"It's only rain," Honey said patiently, brushing off his warnings. She kissed Meagan on the cheek and turned, grabbing her rain hat as she dashed out the door. What was he so worried about? Was he afraid she'd have an accident and he wouldn't be able to cope? Didn't he realize she had done this hundreds of times? She was accustomed to weather like this, having lived in the mercurial Gulf Coast area so long.

The barn creaked ominously from the storm's wrath, but Honey knew the building was sound. Her footsteps echoed loudly in open spaces. With a pitchfork, she stabbed a large, round bale of hay, spreading the load around in a corner of the barn where it would give the hens and the cats a warm place to snuggle.

One of the hens cackled softly from a rafter, flapping its wings in agitation at the storm.

"Shut up, you flea-bitten future feather bed," she muttered, taking another stab at the bale.

Beau McGuire might be a soap opera star, but he had more problems than most. In fact, the glimpse she'd had of *his* life sounded worse than a soap opera!

She paused in her task, leaning for a moment on the pitchfork handle. He certainly was good-looking though, even more so in person than on TV. His face was similar to Adonis, and his body could rival Michelangelo's *David*. But his preppy clothing! That absolutely had to go.

She shook the pitchfork of hay over the corner, letting the dried grass fall like raindrops.

But who was she to judge him? He had every right to be himself, so long as it didn't interfere with her lifestyle. They were all stuck together for at least the next three days unless this hurricane was an exception to the ones before it, so she might as well make the best of it.

Since Peter's death she had been living in near solitary confinement. An occasional party certainly wouldn't label her an extrovert, so having to get along with a handsome soap opera star and his darling but precocious three-year-old would be an enlightening experience for her.

After setting the pitchfork aside, she opened the big wooden barrel by the door, then scattered scratch, the feed she gave the hens, around the middle of the floor. Usually she fed them outside where the small rodents couldn't get at it, but she had no choice right now. The cats would no doubt make sure that even the bravest of the mice wouldn't survive.

Emptying some cat food into a small dish and kicking herself for not bringing out the bowl that held the

kitchen scraps, she finally made her way back to the
barn door facing the house. Four grown cats and six
kittens needed more than the sissy cat food she'd put
out, but it would have to do for the moment. The rain
was really coming down now, and the wind had almost doubled its force since she had entered the barn.

Suddenly she had an idea that sent her back to the
momma cat who was lying in the corner, nursing her
babies. "You won't need one for a little while, will you,
Blackie?" she said softly, disengaging a kitten from its
milk source and cuddling it in the palm of her hand.
Its little eyes were barely open. A tiny pink tongue
licked away a few drops of milk from his black-and-
white face. "This one should do," she said. "She's fat
enough to last a little while without your help."

Tucking the furry bundle carefully under her raincoat, Honey dashed back to the door of the house.
The wind buffeted the screen door as she opened it and
it flew from her hand, slamming against the side of the
house with a resounding whack.

"Are you okay?" Beau stood anxiously just inside
the back door, Meagan in his arms. His frown and
concerned tone confirmed his worry.

"I'm fine," she said lightly, quickly shutting the
door behind her. "Meagan, come see your visitor," she
called as she shed her coat, sitting right down on the
oval rag rug in front of the stove. "She's come to see
you, 'cause she misses you."

Meagan's eyes widened as she recognized the little kitten wobbling around on the floor next to the warmth. She wriggled out of her father's arms and edged slowly over to sit on the rug beside Honey, her eyes as big as her face. "Kitty?" she asked reverently, and Honey nodded.

One tiny plump hand reached out to stroke the fur, her touch as gentle as could be.

Her green eyes looked up. "Mine?"

Honey shook her head. "It belongs to momma cat, but this kitty wanted to come and see you. Do you like her?" The black curls bobbed up and down. "Then very carefully cross your legs, Indian style, like this." Honey demonstrated, and Meagan tried to follow suit. "Put her there so she has a little nest between your legs."

Beau stood watching the scene before him. Meagan. His child. His miracle, and someone else was teaching her new things and sharing new experiences with her. Someone kind and gentle and very loving.

He watched Honey's face soften as she helped Meagan pick up the kitten and place it in her lap. The softness was disconcerting. Shelly had been the only woman in his life who had ever worn that maternal look Honey had now.

For someone so tightly contained and matter-of-fact, this woman showed a great deal of insight.

It was already midmorning, and she still hadn't bothered to put on makeup or do more than twist her hair into a haphazard topknot. He guessed it was her regular habit, but he had nothing to base it on except intuition. Her eyes were clear, her flawless complexion well-scrubbed. Why didn't she wear makeup? Most women he knew were never caught without it, using it as a mask to hide their real selves. This woman was different.

Too different for him to fathom.

Still seated in front of the stove, Honey and Meagan sat on the floor carrying on a low-voiced conversation centered completely on the kitten in Meagan's lap. They had created another, calmer world that somehow excluded him. He felt jealousy beginning to stir until Meagan's eyes sought him out, seeking his approval of her actions as she gently but childishly patted the baby kitten's head. A lump rose to his throat so that all he could do was smile warmly at her.

The silence became companionable, neither Honey nor Beau willing to speak for fear that it might shatter the tenuous feelings of goodwill permeating the room.

Meagan christened the kitten "Sandals," because it loved to chew on her shoes. Reluctantly Honey stood up to return the kitten to its mother. As she put on her raincoat, she kept watching Meagan playing with the kitten.

"May I use your phone?" Beau's deep voice brought her back from her reverie.

"Of course. Use the extension in the living room. You'll be more comfortable." Her lips twitched impishly. "And have I got a phone bill for you," she teased. "It took several calls and a lot of waiting to finally get hold of you."

He chuckled. "It was worth it. And I don't mind paying that bill in the least." He glanced down at his daughter. "Meagan, I'm going to call Shelly. Do you want to talk to her?"

Meagan looked up from the furry bundle in her lap. She shook her head "no" until the dark curls bounced.

As Beau entered the peaceful silence of the living room, he realized for the first time how cozy this house was. It was clean and tidy, with just enough of a mess so that it felt lived in, but not enough to be cluttered.

Seated at Honey's desk, he began dialing. Even though the electricity was out, the phone still operated. Probably not for long. First he'd call Shelly and then the private investigator. Though Meagan was safe, he wanted to know if there had been any further word on Pamela's whereabouts.

4

THE REST OF THE DAY passed uneventfully. The downstairs of the house was well lit by kerosene lamps, and logs were blazing in the fireplace to help dispel the chilly dampness. Honey had called her neighbors and checked on the cattle, which seemed to have no desire to come in out of the rain and head for the dry barn. There was no accounting for bovine judgment.

A stew bubbling on the back burner of the wood stove wafted its spicy aroma through the air. Honey sat in the corner of the room facing her inoperable computer, transcribing by hand number after number onto large accounting sheets. Meagan lay on the floor cutting out paper dolls. Outside the storm continued to vent its fury.

Beau was on the couch, reading anything and everything available. Earlier he had gone out to the car to get his things. He had finally shaved the heavy stubble from his jaw and now looked somewhat less menacing but equally devastating.

Honey couldn't understand her reaction to him at all, and it added to her frustration. Whenever he came close, she shied nervously away, her muscles tense and her heart beating faster. She also felt angry with herself and her response to him. She tried to deny the anger instead of admitting it.

By the time she called Meagan and Beau to dinner and they were all seated at the kitchen table bathed in the golden glow of a hurricane lamp, she had her emotions under control enough to look at Beau without revealing her feelings. *She* wasn't even sure what they were, yet.

"Delicious," Beau said after two or three savory spoonfuls of stew.

"Thank you," she said calmly.

"What do you do with that computer?" he asked curiously. "When the electricity is on, that is."

She looked at him, trying to ignore her reaction. He was far too potent and definitely not made to fit into her life. "I'm an accountant. I keep books for several small businesses in the area. Some of the ranches and horse farms even use me to double-check their own systems."

His brows rose. "An accountant?"

Honey nodded. "Why? Is there something wrong with accountants?"

"No, I . . ." he began, and stopped. "I'm just surprised, that's all. You don't look like any accountant I've ever seen." His piercing green eyes drifted over her face and down her neck, halting at the soft curves of her breasts. The sweater was bulky, but nothing could have hidden their fullness.

"We come in all shapes and sizes." The minute the words escaped, she knew she shouldn't have said them, and her blush proved it.

He gave a lazy chuckle, his eyes gleaming an even deeper hue as he noted her discomfort. "Apparently. And I'd say your numbers are perfect," he added, tongue in cheek, a hint of mischief in his tone.

"I've had my own business for a long time," she said, attempting to recover her poise by pretending she hadn't noticed his appreciative glance or heard his seductive comment.

"I certainly wasn't doubting your ability, Honey," he said quietly. "Have you always lived here?"

Honey sighed, leaning back. She was becoming tense again and she knew it. She wasn't used to talking about herself and didn't like his searching questions, knowing what he would eventually ask. She took a deep breath and tried to relax. "Yes. This used to be my parents' property. I was born in a little clinic in Tomball, a town about seven miles east of here, and I was raised on this land."

"Was your husband from here, too?"

"No." There it was, the question she had been waiting for. She glanced down at the half-eaten bowl of stew in front of her, attempting to avoid his penetrating gaze. "We met in college. He was from the Memorial area in Houston, so he was accustomed to traffic jams, fast-food restaurants on every corner and discos on the weekends." She knew she sounded cool and controlled, but her heart was aching at the recollection of Peter.

"This kind of life must have been quite a switch for him," Beau commented, his eyes narrowing as he studied her response.

"Not at first, because we lived in the city then. It wasn't until my parents died that we moved out here."

"Did he enjoy it as much as you seem to?"

She met his level gaze. "What is this? Twenty questions?"

Carefully he placed his spoon next to his plate and leaned back, his eyes riveted on her face. "No. Merely curiosity." His voice was soft but firm, and she thought he would have made a terrific cross-examining attorney.

Honey leaned back, too. The sadness in her eyes had warned him that she didn't really want to be the topic of discussion. "Then let me appease it for you, by all means," she said as calmly as she could. "My husband hated the country life as much as I loved it. Frankly, I don't know if he ever would have loved it because he never had much of a chance to find out. He was killed in a car accident on the freeway in Houston during rush hour."

All her pent-up loneliness and heartache poured out in those few words.

"I'm sorry," was all he said, but it was enough.

She closed her eyes to the thoughts that seemed to jam her mind. "I'm sorry, too," she said hollowly.

The rest of the meal was eaten in silence except for Meagan's chattering about Sandals, the kitten.

When they were finished, Beau began to clear the table.

"I'll do that," Honey said, breaking into Meagan's monologue. "You go ahead and relax."

"I don't mind helping." He stood there, a plate in each hand as his eyes probed hers.

"No," she insisted. "Please, I'd rather do them myself."

"Are you all right?"

She tried to smile for Meagan's sake. "I'm fine. Just take care of Meagan, will you?"

Reluctantly he walked out of the door, holding Meagan's hand as they went into the living room.

Honey began heating water, praying she wouldn't replay the memories that threatened to immerse her in the past. She had to keep busy. To stay busy.

Meagan kept them both occupied that evening, dancing to music from the transistor radio. She even got Beau to dance with her once or twice and inveigled Honey into hopping like a bunny and turning somersaults. By the time Meagan's bedtime rolled around, Beau and Honey were as tired as Meagan. But at least, thanks to the little one's childish antics, the tension that had burgeoned during and after dinner had evaporated.

Beau put Meagan to bed while Honey straightened up downstairs. She was putting away cups in the kitchen when she heard him come down again and go into the living room.

She didn't need to hear his footsteps to know he was near; Honey would have known that because her skin tingled every time he got within a yard of her. She fiddled with odds and ends, trying to delay the moment when she would have to join him. But there was only so much work to do, and when the coffee cups and milk glass had been cleaned and dried, she couldn't put off his company any longer.

Honey stopped, the kerosene lamp in her hand, when she reached the living room doorway, staring at the tall, broad-shouldered man who was pouring himself a drink at the bar. Another lamp was at his elbow, its light combining with the firelight and reflecting off his tanned face. If the pinched look around his mouth was anything to go by, he was exhausted. Who wouldn't be if his child had been missing for a week, and when he'd finally located her, couldn't return home because of a violent hurricane? What surprised her was that, even though he was worn out, a raw virility surrounded him, nudging her sensual awareness of him to a heightened pitch.

"I might have a few ice cubes left, if you'd like some," she said, her voice Southern soft.

He turned, swirling his glass of straight whiskey, his green eyes unfathomable in the dim light. Looking down, he watched the golden-brown liquid revolving in his glass. "No, thanks. This will be fine."

An awkward silence filled the room as Honey went over to the couch, placed the lamp on the side table and sat down to reach for a magazine. She flipped through the gaily colored pages, but all her senses were finely tuned toward the man standing by the bar.

He was much too handsome, almost a storybook version of Prince Charming, and his eyes were far too green. His massive shoulders and small waist and hips belonged to a *Gentlemen's Quarterly* fashion model. Most obvious of all to her was his attitude. He seemed to be studying her reaction to everything. His apparent analysis of her was the most nerve-racking experience she had ever had.

She looked up to find his eyes on her once more. "Do you always stare at people like that?"

"Not always, but you're an interesting subject," he said slowly, weighing his words.

"An interesting subject for what?" She was intrigued by his statement despite herself.

"The study of a complex human. It's my business to portray characters and understand their motives," he explained, his eyes dissecting her. "Each of us has many different motives that make us speak and act as we do. I've been trying to figure out yours."

For the first time she laughed. The deep throaty sound seemed to ruffle his skin and nerves, and he almost recoiled from the feeling. "Oh, Beau, you really are barking up the wrong tree. Why, I'm as simple as they come. I can't be much of a challenge to you."

"Really? Then maybe you should see yourself from my point of view. I see a woman who finds a child in the back seat of her car—"

"Van," Honey corrected.

"Van at three a.m., and instead of calling the police, as most people would, she trusts the person who wrote a name and number on an unsigned note, and she calls it. Then she takes superb care of the abandoned child while she awaits the arrival of someone to take over for her. Meanwhile, she runs, single-handedly, an accounting business, a house and a goodly amount of land with lots of animals on it. She wears no makeup. Her hairstyle is simplicity itself—straight or in a bun. And her clothing detracts instead of attracts. She also has an invisible radar that goes off if a man steps within a three-foot radius. Oh, yes, and she sips her whiskey neat."

Her magazine plopped onto the floor, but Honey wasn't aware of it. "My God," she said wonderingly. "Is that how you see me? And I don't drink whiskey. I barely touched my glass, if you recall. Anyway, that's the only bottle of liquor still left over from . . . past days."

"I have more to say." His eyes bored into hers, the thousands questions he had almost visible in his expression. "Much more. That was barely scratching the surface."

Honey shook her head, denying him. "Don't tell me," she said in a low voice. Her eyes widened. Was she so simple or so transparent that he could easily read her thoughts and dreams and emotions?

"Why?"

"Because I don't want to know. Your opinion is just that, Beau. One opinion."

He studied her. She wasn't being coy or playing games. "I'm sorry," he said finally. "That was just a parlor game, something I do at cocktail parties to pass the time." He shrugged and tossed her a casual grin, showing he didn't care. "It's cheaper than going to a psychiatrist."

The tension left her slowly. "And do you attend many parties?"

"Every weekend. In New York, especially in this business, it's a necessity." His expression hardened at the thought as he took a sip of his drink. "What about you?"

"Not very often," she admitted. "I was at a client's party the night I found Meagan in my van, but I'm not much for socializing. Everything I enjoy is right here."

"Then I'll always be thankful you went to that party. Someone else might have called the police and then the whole sordid mess would have been splashed all over TV and the gossip papers. And that would have been very hard on both Meagan and me."

"I thought you liked publicity."

"Not when it concerns Meagan. I want my family life as quiet and private and normal as possible. For all our sakes." His voice was velvety. "Just like you, Honey."

She was silent a moment, then got to her feet. "Well, good night, Beau," she said. "As enlightening as this conversation has been, morning comes early here."

"Won't you have one drink with me if I promise not to play any more parlor games?"

The only one she had ever played had been spin the bottle in grade school. Somehow she thought he'd feel that one was a bit tame, no matter how much she would like to have felt his lips caressing hers.

She shook her head, hardening herself against his coaxing. "I know I must seem a bit countrified to you, but there's really a lot to do here in the early morning." She moved toward the doorway, edging closer to the dark stairs. "I'd better take a quick sponge bath and go to bed."

"The country mouse," he said softly, as if confirming another observation. Then he tossed back the rest of his drink.

Her eyes shot golden-brown sparks as she stood taller with his every word. That remark hurt all the more because she secretly believed that it fit. "Better that than the city mouse—a role I never could fill," she replied before exiting the room, walking slowly up the stairs. She hadn't really wanted to leave him, but he made her feel so inept at carrying on a sophisticated conversation.

Her remark seemed to amuse him, almost as if he could read her mind and see the contradictions there. "Good night, Honey," he called after her, amusement tinging his voice.

Finding her way in the dark, she reached the safety of the bedroom and closed the door with a loud click.

When the door slipped noisily in place, Meagan jumped and Honey realized she had forgotten all about the small child. She should have closed the door much more gently. "Go back to sleep, sweetheart. I'm just getting ready to join you," she whispered.

Meagan nodded groggily, and her eyes closed again as she drifted quickly back into slumber. Honey lit a candle that was sitting on the dresser, watching it throw out just enough dim light to dance willowy golden shadows on the wall.

The din of the raging storm outside seemed to lull instead of frighten her as she stared out the window, unable to see the ground for the continuous sheets of rain.

She finally turned away, pulling at the pins in her hair and dropping them on the dresser as she loosened the topknot. With her fingertips, she massaged her temple, hoping the subtle ache there would go away. Then she slipped the sweater over her head and unbuttoned her blouse, allowing it to drop from her shoulders and over her hands. She hadn't bothered to wear a bra, and when the damp night air touched her bare skin, her nipples puckered.

She heard the knob rattle lightly first, then her bedroom door opened and a flashlight shone on her face and bare breasts.

Both their gasps were audible, but neither one moved or spoke. Time seemed to stand still as Beau stood framed in the doorway, his face in shadows, the flashlight trained on the naked top half of her body. She could feel the light on her skin as if it were the merest of touches, and its faint heat seemed to permeate her body until it curled around and settled in her lower abdomen.

Honey was frozen in place. She closed her eyes against the glare, then swallowed hard, her hands stiff at her sides. "Get out," she finally managed in a low voice. Anger and humiliation were warring inside her, along with an unbelievably heady excitement that seemed to singe her nerve endings.

At first he didn't move, then the beam lowered toward the floor. "I . . . I was just checking on Meagan. I thought you were in the bathroom," he said thickly. "I'm sorry." The door clicked shut once more.

Honey shivered in reaction. Folding her arms over her breasts, she stared at the closed door. Why hadn't she covered herself instead of just standing there, her body paralyzed? Why hadn't she done as she had said she would and taken a bath?

She slipped a worn flannel gown over her head and stepped out of her jeans, shucking off her shoes at the same time. In seconds she was tucked in bed, curled into a tight, protective ball.

She listened as the storm lashed around them, hoping, no, praying that it would end soon and Mr. Beau McGuire would be able to leave. He was a man with a power that drew her to him against her will. And it wasn't going to do her any good. He was out of her league, and she knew it.

Her only regret was losing Meagan's companionship when the storm ended, but even that was overshadowed by her intense and puzzling feelings toward the child's father.

For no reason, tears oozed slowly from her eyes to dampen the pillow beneath her head. She sniffled once, then fell asleep.

Dreams of things that had been promised and never come true danced through her head to haunt her. The tears continued to dampen the pillow without her being aware of them.

WHEN HONEY OPENED HER EYES, the next morning, Meagan was already gone. She sat up, listening for sounds of activity, but all she heard was the intense wind knocking at the house for entrance.

Her head really hurt. Her throat felt sore and her muscles were cramped. She grimaced, realizing that was what came of sleeping so tensely in a fetal position.

By the time she opened her bedroom door, she was dressed and ready to face the day—and Beau. In the clear light of day she was sure her reaction to the previous night's peep show was just a plain old case of nerves. Beau had certainly been as shocked as she. And he had probably been telling the truth and had just come in to check on Meagan. The whole incident had been a dumb move on both their parts. She ignored the other feelings that seemed to be at war inside her.

The aroma of brewing coffee greeted her the minute her foot hit the landing. Strong, fragrant . . . and burnt. Beau obviously didn't know the first thing about making coffee on a wood stove.

She smiled as she paused unnoticed in the kitchen doorway. Her smile nearly became outright laughter.

Meagan sat at the table, staring down at a plate of milky scrambled eggs and blackened toast with a disgusted expression. Just then, Beau reached for the aluminum coffeepot only to scorch his fingers.

"Damn," he growled under his breath, grabbing a towel and wrapping it quickly around the handle. Then he tried again, barely managing to slide the pot from one burner to another.

"Need some help?" Honey asked, barely able to keep a giggle out of her voice. Any worries about how she would act this morning after the confrontation last night fled from her mind.

"Daddy's burning everything," Meagan said, wrinkling her nose as she slipped out of her seat and into Honey's arms. "Uggh." Her sound fit perfectly Honey's description of the child's breakfast.

Honey winked at her, earning a baby chuckle in reply, which only seemed to irritate Beau more, if the look he shot over his shoulder was any indication.

"I'm not sure, but I think I made the fire too hot, added too much wood or left open too many vents," Beau said with strained patience as he rinsed his hand with a glass of cold water.

"Meaning you could cook if it was electric?" Honey inquired innocently as she sat Meagan back down in front of her breakfast and reached for the bread to make more toast.

"Of course. If you'll remember, I had no problem making eggs yesterday, er, after you lit the stove."

Honey smiled and said nothing as she put several slices of bread on the oven rack and shut the door. She scraped the rest of the undercooked eggs into the bowl for the cats and started fresh, opening two vents on the sides of the old stove to regulate the temperature.

In minutes she had cooked and served a fluffy omelet and buttered toast. Beau watched her slide the omelet onto a plate, then slice off a small portion for Meagan. Honey sat down across from him, trying hard not to smirk. She glanced at him through her lashes, hoping she wouldn't get caught trying to gauge his reaction. But she was.

A lazy, satisfied smile lifted the corners of his mouth, and deep laugh lines fanned out from his eyes. No doubt about it—he was devastating.

"Proud of yourself, aren't you?" His deep voice stilled her hand in midair.

"Proud of what?"

"Proud that you could show me just how efficient you are."

Meagan kept right on eating, but her big green eyes flitted between Honey and her father, her interest apparent.

"Yes," she said conversationally when she could finally swallow her bite of toast. "It's always nice to verify that one is good at something."

His brows lifted in surprise, his eyes deepening to a mysterious fern green. He had been expecting games and denials, but instead he got the truth. "You're a good cook," he finally admitted.

Honey nodded. "I know. I'm also a good accountant."

"Do you always toot your own horn?"

She thought he was being sarcastic, but when she looked up she realized he was teasing her. "If I don't, who will?" Her tone told him that he had finally touched the right chord for debate. She was fun to talk to, to discuss things with.

"Your customers?"

She smiled sweetly. "But they're not here, Beau. I am."

"Touché," he said softly with a smile winning an even more sincere smile from her.

"Besides, don't you get your name in the paper for the same reason? To remind people of your acting ability—tooting *your* own horn?"

He nodded slowly. "Yes." His eyes narrowed, but she could see mirth there. "Are you sure you're not a lawyer?"

She grinned. Earlier she'd thought that he would have made a good attorney. "Nope, just a lowly numbers cruncher."

"Lowly, my foot," he murmured, imitating her drawl as they smiled at each other, sharing unspoken thoughts, yet connecting somehow.

"Daddy, I want to paint." Meagan yanked on her father's sleeve, breaking the spell and demanding his attention.

Honey stood quickly, reaching for the empty toast plate. "Good idea, Meagan. While you paint and your father does the dishes, I'll go feed the animals."

"Dishes?" Beau said cautiously. "How? We don't have any water."

She pointed toward the corner where the buckets and bottles were lined up. "Sure you do. There. Just heat it up and start scrubbing."

The green eyes narrowed. "You're kidding."

At the kitchen door, she slipped on the slicker hanging there, deliberately not looking at him for fear of laughing. Then she stepped into her high rubber boots. "I'm sure you'll do fine." She crammed the rainhat onto her head, pulling it down as far as it would go. Today the storm was really raging; it would be another day or two before the wind died down.

With her hand on the doorknob, she turned to Beau who was still sitting at the kitchen table. The remnants of a smile still curled her lips as she admonished him. "Since you made most of the mess, you can clean it up. Just don't waste too much water. I won't be able to borrow a portable generator from one of the neighbors for a few days."

"Generator?"

Honey sighed, their easy camaraderie quickly disappearing. Was this man from another planet or only another city? "Yes, a portable generator. My water is pumped from a well in the ground and held in a large metal tank in one of the sheds. Nothing works without electricity. To pump more water, I have to borrow a portable generator to produce electricity." This time she raised her brows. "Any other questions?"

Beau mumbled something under his breath as he took his plate to the counter, but Honey couldn't make out what he said because she was too busy laughing to herself as she left the safety of the house to face the hurricane.

Beau began heating the water, his mumblings unheeded by Meagan as she sat with paper and a paint set, drawing pastel colors from one end of the sheet to the other. Her concentration was so intense that the tip of her little pink tongue came out to tickle her up-per lip as her dark brows pushed together from her effort.

By the time the water had heated and he began to wash the dishes, Beau was grinning again.

Okay, so she had asked him to work. He wasn't upset at being asked to share the load; it was just her way of doing things was so foreign to him. She might have chosen something else for him to do, like chop-ping wood or moving furniture . . . but she had cho-sen this, as if she wanted to be perverse and believed he had no experience with such mundane matters. His grin broadened. How many thousands of dishes had he washed when he'd been struggling, waiting for his big break? But washing them country-style by heat-ing water on a wood stove that definitely hated him—well, that was another matter.

But he couldn't blame her. Through circumstances beyond either of their control, she was their hostess during the hurricane.

Finally he chuckled aloud. No one he knew in New York would have dared to tell him anything, let alone order him to do kitchen chores.

His eyes darted to the kitchen window. The barn was a smoky shadow against the darkness of the swirling rain. Honey was just walking through the barn door, and he had to smile. In that slicker, rubber boots and a wide-brimmed hat, she could be mis-taken for any cowboy out doing ranch chores. He would have thought that she might have cared more about her appearance. Maybe living out in the country with only a few neighbors had made her careless.

But he knew better. Last night, when he had shone the flashlight at her, his breath had literally caught in his throat. Pure energy had seemed to rush through his system so fast that he had become paralyzed. A heavy lead had plummeted into the pit of his stomach, and he'd known that any move he made would simply have propelled him toward her to gather her into his arms.

Her breasts were flawless—full and slightly curving so that the nipples were tilted upward. Her gently sloping shoulders were much smaller than he had imagined. Her expression had been as stunned as his. He couldn't move a muscle, his reaction had been so powerful. When she'd growled at him to get out, he had finally come back to life. He might have stood there all night if she hadn't spoken and broken the spell.

A familiar tightening in his loins had reminded him he surely couldn't have stood that much pressure. He definitely would have taken her into his arms and crushed her perfectly formed body to his. What was disconcerting was that for several seconds he had forgotten Meagan was in the room, that there was a storm outside and that he had other commitments and another life.

At that moment though, he had wanted Honey with a passion he had never known with other women. For the space of several seconds, desire, base sexual desire, had inundated him, taking away his breath, his muscle control, his very sanity. At the same time he had felt an overpowering need to protect her. He had wanted to hold her securely in his arms and never let her go. He had never felt that way before.

His smile dissolved into a frown. He never wanted to feel like that again. Especially not with Honey. It was all too intense.

Glancing out the window again, he attempted to peer through the fuzzy wall the rain created. What the hell did she actually do out there?

"Daddy," Meagan called, holding up her latest masterpiece and awaiting his reaction.

This time, when his heart swelled, it was for the pure love of his daughter. He gave her a hug. "It's beautiful, sweetheart," he said, remembering how close he had come to losing her. If anything had happened to his little girl, there wouldn't have been a stone left unturned until he had found Pamela and made her pay.

Sighing, he kissed the top of Meagan's curly head. Then he flashed her another grin. "Just beautiful."

"I love you," she said, whispering in his ear and reminding him of their own private form of communication, which had begun when she was an infant. He would give her a hug and whisper those words as if they were a secret just between the two of them.

It didn't matter that he was a single parent; he was determined she would receive all the love he could give, making sure she'd never have cause to regret her mother not being there for her.

Looking at her now, he knew that so far he had succeeded—with a lot of help from his sister. Shelly would graduate from college next month, no simple accomplishment considering she had taken over so much of Meagan's care so he could pursue his career. She would soon be imparting her love for physical science to junior high students. Shelly had truly been a godsend.

They both wanted Meagan to have the best start in life they could provide. Meagan was healthy, happy and loved. Wasn't that what was important? His heart told him yes.

Meagan and Shelly and his career were all that counted for him in this world. Everything else could go to hell, as long as he had them by his side.

And certainly no woman who dressed like a man, sometimes talked like a sailor and thought like an accountant needed to have anything to do with his orderly life.

HONEY TRAMPED THROUGH the newly forked hay, scuffing her feet so that she could kick up any eggs rather than stepping on them. The guineas, thank goodness, had been in the barn ever since the storm had started. They didn't have sense enough to stay out of the rain unless they were locked in. The dumb things would stand there and drown with their beaks open while they watched the heavens pour. But they made the best darn alarm system in the world when the weather was nice, cackling and crowing whenever a stranger came down her long driveway or tried to enter the yard.

Digging into the feed barrel with an old dented pot, she scattered scratch across the floor.

The cat and kittens had fresh water and a few pouches of cat food that she kept on hand for emergencies. Everything was done.

Making sure the barn door was secured, she bent her head and made her way slowly toward the house, wishing for the first time that the barn had been built closer.

A kerosene lamp shone through the kitchen window like a beacon for the cold, wet world outside. Inside was Beau McGuire, everybody's heartthrob. Wouldn't her neighbors be jealous if they knew he was here! They'd probably tramp over in droves just for a glimpse of the handsome hunk, hurricane or no!

But he certainly wasn't for her. The nearly overwhelming feelings that had assailed her last night weren't really because of him; they were just the bittersweet reactions of a woman who had lived alone for the past few years. And that was all, she reassured herself, denying that she hadn't known that feeling since—well, in a long time. She had to believe her response was the result of cutting herself off from everyone except her clients, not even bothering to have a social life anymore. A creature of habit . . .

Besides, city mice were a dime a dozen. Not one compared favorably with the real security of her land. Her land. Now that was real. It housed her, fed her, gave her a sense of purpose and accomplishment nothing and no one could ever take away. The land was her saving grace.

None of the men she had ever known had been able to give her what this land had provided.

She held on to the screen door and placed her hand on the doorknob. For some reason that she didn't quite understand, she hesitated, peering through the window first instead of opening the door.

Beau was bent over Meagan, giving her a hug that spoke eloquently of his love for her. His eyes were squeezed shut, his hand gently cradling Meagan's curly head against his broad shoulder.

But the one tiny movement that put a knot in her throat was Meagan's pudgy little hands as they patted her father's back in solace. It was almost as if she knew she was her father's rock and he needed her for comfort.

They had each other.

A wave of pure envy shot through Honey as she stood there silently, staring like a voyeur into another person's most private life. Unexpected tears clouded her eyes and still she stared, unable to stop herself. Her eyes ate up all the love she viewed, making her ache all over with the notion that while she could recognize love well enough, she had none of her own.

Her hand tightened on the knob, and she twisted it open, walking in quickly and slamming the door to keep out the driving wind and rain.

"Still pretty bad, isn't it?" Beau asked as he stood up, lifting Meagan in his arms. Her little hands were on his shoulders, her green eyes even bigger than her daddy's. Her smile was brilliant.

"Yes," she answered, talking past the lump in her throat. She had been alone for a long time, but this was the first time she ever remembered being so *lonely*.

"How long do you think this storm will last?"

"Another day, maybe two." Again her answer was to the point.

She took off the slicker and hung it back on the peg, then slipped off her boots. Turning she found his eyes on her, and her heart skipped a beat. She walked with jerky steps to the cabinet and lifted a mug from the shelf, keeping her back to him as she fought to regain control.

When she heard Meagan's sandals patter out the kitchen door toward the living room, she knew they were alone. Taking a deep breath, she decided to face him.

Her golden-flecked eyes challenged his as she stared defiantly at him, her chin tilted slightly. His green eyes narrowed, taking in the tenseness of her expression, drifting down to study curiously the rapid rise and fall of her breasts. At last he stared pointedly at the hands gripping the cup, and when he spoke his question shocked her.

"Are you afraid of me, Honey? Afraid I might harm you in some way?" he asked her quietly.

"Isn't that a little farfetched?" She turned back to the stove and poured herself half a cup of coffee.

He slowly shook his head, his eyes searching out hers once more. "No, I think it's a perfectly natural reaction. You've lived alone for a long time. When a stranger comes into your home and shares it so thoroughly, you're bound to be wary. Especially when that person plays a self-centered playboy on TV. Many people confuse the characters actors play with the actors themselves."

She shook her head. "That's ridiculous," she croaked, covering up her shaken nerves by sipping coffee. It could have been arsenic for all that she could taste.

His brows shot up. "Why? You're a very attractive woman, and I seem to affect you in some way. It occured to me that maybe you're frightened of me. But if that's not it, what is it?"

Golden flecks of fire lasered toward him, and he knew for the first time that the trite expression "if looks could kill" fit this moment perfectly. "If you're trying to suggest that I'm a lonely widow desperate for some entertainment, you can think again." Her slight body stiffened with every word she bit off.

His chest expanded slowly as he breathed in deeply. Everyone needed defenses, and she obviously needed hers now.

"Either you've been badly hurt or you're terrified of something," he said quietly. "Either way you don't need to fear me. I won't hurt you. Hell, I don't even know you." He paused, trying to control the urgent need to know her better. "Besides, lady, you're just not my type," he finally lied, punctuating the statement with a twisted, wry smile.

Honey's mouth opened to argue, to get him as stirred up as she was whenever he was around her.

But he'd left the room.

5

HONEY DIDN'T SEE BEAU the rest of the day, which was fine with her—and a balm for her nervous system. She was having enough trouble controlling her emotions around him. But hardest of all was accepting that she was truly drawn to him. Hadn't she learned anything the last time she rode the merry-go-round of love? The most painful thing in the world was to reach for the prized brass ring, only to fall flat on your face. She was out of her depth, and she knew it.

Beau stayed in one room, while she paced back and forth in another. She was embarrassed by her outburst, but the words that would form an apology kept getting scrambled in her head. She was confused, too, by her intense physical reaction to him whenever he was near. She kept telling herself that it was nothing but pure lust. And who wouldn't be attracted to someone as good-looking as Beau? But there was more to it than that.

She did some of her accounting worksheets since she couldn't use the computer. Running over the figures and organizing them logically was a form of release that consumed her thoughts. In a way it was

cleansing. Even when the world didn't work right and
straight and clean, the numbers did. They were always perfect, adding and subtracting to the same answer every time.

Only humans had a built-in error factor; humans
didn't always know the right answers or how to find
them.

At four o'clock she put down her pencil and turned
off the small hand-held calculator. Flexing her
cramped writing hand, she stared out the living room
window.

When the rain and wind were gone, Beau would
leave, taking Meagan with him. Then her life would
return to normal, to the routine she knew so well and
acted out by rote, having done it for the past three
years. Her life was safe, expecting no more of her than
she was used to. It was very comfortable.

For the first time that she could recall, another
thought slipped into her mind like floodwater seeping under a door. It was also boring.

She propped her chin in her hand. But wasn't that
what she wanted? Something she could count on
when everything and everyone else in the world was
spinning so chaotically?

Meagan's laughter floated down the stairs to curl
around her, highlighting once more that she was used
to a solitary life. By choice or by chance.

She stood up, suddenly impatient for action, for
something physical to do, and she headed toward the

kitchen. Come hurricane or Beau McGuire, she still had meals to cook.

BEAU SAT ON THE EDGE of his bed in the guest room, his hands resting on his thighs as he watched Meagan play with a new set of paper dolls that Honey had got her before he had arrived. It had taken them all afternoon to cut them out and match the clothes to Princess Di and Charles, because Megan was sure the Princess would love to wear pants and shirts. Honey's influence on Meagan had been swift and certain.

He watched his daughter without really seeing, his mind replaying the scene in the kitchen that morning. Didn't that damn woman realize that he had the best-looking women in New York falling over themselves just to spend one night in his bed? He didn't need a woman, any woman, and he didn't like the feeling that Honey was on the alert, just waiting for him to attack her, to ravish her body, and then forget she ever existed. What could she be thinking of?

And why did he have such a strong urge to attack? Of all people, he knew the value of softly spoken words aimed so true. When he had said she wasn't his type, he had known how much that would hurt her. Not because she cared about being his type, but because what he'd said was an insult aimed straight at her ego.

That wasn't like him. Pamela had said similar things to him during their times together, and even in his frustration he had promised himself he would never undermine another human being as she had tried to undermine him.

He sighed. This woman was an enigma. And someone to definitely stay away from.

If only he could erase the vivid image of her, standing there so defiantly, so frightened yet beautifully naked from the waist up.

DINNER WAS a quiet affair. Honey had grilled two T-bone steaks and had baked three perfect fluffy potatoes. The food sat in the center of the table, the potatoes steaming and dripping with butter and melted cheese. She had also made some lightly steamed broccoli picked from her garden just days before.

They sat around the table, enclosed in the golden rays of the kerosene lamp. If everything had been normal, they would have looked like an average family sitting down to dinner. Instead, there was a tension in the air that thickened so that there was almost no room left to breathe.

"Pass the salt, please," Beau said. Honey complied.

"Still nasty weather outside," Honey murmured a few minutes later.

Beau nodded.

The electric light over the kitchen sink flickered on, then went off again. Meagan drew a sharp breath, delight dawning on her face. Once more the lights pulsed, then dimmed into darkness.

"Well," Honey remarked brightly. "At least someone's out there trying."

"Lights?" Meagan asked wistfully.

"Not yet, sweetheart. But soon," Beau said, his eyes riveted on Honey. When the lights had flickered, he had seen her become animated, unguarded, and that picture was engraved in his mind. God, she was beautiful.

"Beau?" Honey was glancing at him strangely. He seemed to be looking at her, but she wasn't sure. Actually, he seemed to be looking right through her.

He shook his head. "I'm sorry. What?"

"Are you all right?" Her real concern colored her voice and turned his insides into warm dough. Her soft slight drawl seeped into him like warm molasses.

"Fi—" He cleared his voice, astonished at his reaction to her. "I'm fine."

Honey watched him carefully for a while, staring at him through her thick, lowered lashes. When she couldn't take the strained silence anymore, she spoke up. "So tell me," she began, "what's your day like when you're in New York?"

"Why?" He registered surprise at her interest, and she blushed. While it was true she had asked only the barest of personal questions before, her curiosity had to be appeased sometime.

She smiled, and he almost caught his breath at the sheer beauty of her. "Because you know about my days now. So I thought I'd learn something about yours," she said brightly.

For a moment he couldn't quite focus on the question. Hoping that single dimple would appear again, he couldn't force his eyes to leave her face. He felt an overpowering urge to touch the dimple with his lips. "My day? It's really boring to an outsider. I leave for work at five-thirty in the morning. I memorize my script for the day, go to makeup and wardrobe, block out and walk through the scenes several times, discuss any dialogue that needs to be changed. Then we tape. After we tape, we begin on the next day's scenes. If I'm lucky, I'm home by six in the evening."

His account must not have been too boring; she still looked interested. "And then what?"

"Then I play with Meagan, we all eat, and I always put Meagan to bed." He hesitated as if reluctant to reveal any more information.

"Then Daddy goes out," Meagan piped up, her mouth fill of potatoes.

Beau smiled down at his daughter. "Then Daddy goes out—sometimes," he amended. "I go because it's expected of me, because I have a career that needs constant exposure to continue. At least it does until I'm solidly established."

"Sounds very...jet-setty," Honey said, a faint touch of envy evident.

"Those evenings out are as much a part of my business as the days."

"It must be hectic," she said before the delightful dimple finally appeared. "You poor thing."

Beau was mesmerized as he noticed the animation she revealed when she was at ease. She was like a completely different woman....

When a horn blared through the rain and intruded into the room, they all jumped. But Honey was fastest, running to the back door and pulling it open as a huge man climbed down from the cab of a large open-bed truck.

"Mac!" she cried as she pushed open the screen door for him, her expression one of delighted surprise.

The tall man tramped up the steps and slipped inside the door. As he entered, he bent down, sliding a friendly kiss along her cheek as he removed his plastic-sheathed Stetson. "Hi, Honey. I finally tinkered with that old generator I had in the barn until it started working. Since I've got a new one, I thought you might like to use it." He stopped, his black eyes narrowing as he took in the scene. "Donna said you'd probably go crazy without electricity to work your newfangled computer machine."

Beau and Meagan sat at the table staring back. Meagan inched closer to her father as she craned her neck to take in all of the immense stranger.

Honey grinned quickly at them before introducing her neighbor and good friend. "Oh, Beau and Meagan, I want you to meet my neighbor, Mac. He lives two farms away and is a godsend when a piece of machinery breaks. Mac, Beau McGuire and his daughter, Meagan. They're from New York, but they got caught in our hurricane."

The two men sized each other up, and neither seemed to find the other lacking. As if to seal their judgments, they shook hands and mumbled greetings.

Honey could barely contain her laughter as she watched them. The men were like two roosters in the same barnyard. A typical male reaction, no matter where or which hen.

"Are you a giant?" Meagan asked, kneeling on her chair, but leaning toward her dad for protection.

"I been called a lot of things, little lady, but that ain't one of 'em." Mac chuckled and smiled at the little girl, then glanced back to Beau. "How did you two find Honey's place? Get stranded?" Mac's voice sounded natural enough, even though his eyes dug deeper than his words.

Beau's expression still revealed his curiosity about the big man, but his answer was as bland as sauce without spice. "Honey took care of Meagan for a few days while I finished up some work I had to do. When I got here, there was a storm and it was too late to leave." Beau gave an easy smile, his eyes crinkling at the corners.

"Well, now, that's really nice that you have some visitors to while away the inside time, Honey," Mac drawled, his broad smile widening even more as he gazed at her fondly. "I know you always get antsy with nothing to do."

Honey chuckled. He knew she really enjoyed her solitude and seldom ventured out for company. "You're a rascal, Mac," she said, reaching for a beer in the quilt-covered refrigerator. She pulled the tab and handed it to him.

He took the can without blinking an eye. "Thanks," he said, before sucking it dry in several huge gulps.

In the stunned silence, Mac crushed the can and tossed it into a paper bag under the counter. "Now, let's see if this here generator is fixed as good as I think it is," he muttered, slipping back into his slicker and hat. "Meet me in the barn, sweetie."

Honey quickly grabbed her slicker, shoving her arms into the sleeves. She welcomed some fresh air and escaping from those dark green eyes that seemed to absorb her every movement.

As she stepped outside, she drew a deep breath. For reasons that she refused to delve into, she felt almost claustrophobic around Beau McGuire. Nothing like that occurred with Mac, so it wasn't just any male that affected her so acutely.

They took only a half hour to hook up the generator in the barn. Power would be limited, but at least the hot water heater and the well pump would work, and the quilts could be taken off the refrigerator and freezer. They'd also have light.

As she and Mac stood just inside the open door of the barn, Honey rose on tiptoe and gave the big man a chaste kiss on the cheek. "Thanks, Mac. You don't know how wonderful it will be to have a long hot bath."

"No problem," he said gruffly. "You know how Donna gets all over my hide if I don't take care of you proper-like. She worries about you as if you were her own."

Honey chuckled. Donna, Mac's wife, had taken over the job of mothering her when her best friend, Honey's mother had died. "She was born to be a broody hen."

Mac joined her laughter, and his old eyes twinkled, the delight he still found in his tiny wife obvious. "Hell," he drawled, "she even mothers me after thirty-five years." Then his eyes turned somber once more. "But with a stud like that around the house, I don't think you need mothering. More like a chaperone."

Her brown eyes widened in surprise. Mac had never said anything like that to her! "He's just a friend."

Mac's eyes narrowed suspiciously. "And his daughter?"

"Meagan is adorable, and I think I'm half in love with her, but she leaves when he does," she explained, and he nodded in understanding.

"They may not leave soon enough, Honey. He's eyeing you as if you were the last steak in the meat department."

"That's just plain ridiculous," she insisted, ignoring the flash of emotions that jolted through her in response to Mac's comment. "As a matter of fact I've been informed that I'm not his type."

Mac's eyes crinkled. "A real connoisseur, huh? Doesn't he know that pure gold doesn't always come in fancy city wrappings?"

She shook her head ruefully. Dear Mac. Always there to support her. No matter what. "He's a soap opera star in New York, Mac. He's used to all the glitter and glamour, and to women throwing themselves at his feet."

Mac chuckled, and the sound rumbled up from his chest like thunder. "That's okay, I'll take the country mouse every time. You're a survivor, Honey, and you'll always make it."

The good-humored gleam faded from her eyes. Oh, yes. She was a survivor, all right. Her being here alone proved that. But couldn't she have just a little of the glitter that some country mice had?

"Thanks, Mac. I really appreciate this." Her chin tilted, and he recognized her signal that the discussion had ended.

"You're welcome. Come by and see us when this storm quits. I want to show you some new seed catalogs that just came in."

"Will do," she promised, walking him to his truck despite the rain pouring over them.

By the time she had reached the kitchen and shed her wet clothing, she was exhausted. This new routine that Beau and Megan had projected into her placid life was more tiring that she had thought. Living by herself, she had always known what needed doing and when. Having others around at close range was another matter altogether.

Beau's arms were in suds up to his elbows as he glanced over his shoulder. "Has the big cowboy left?" His voice was faintly derisive.

"Yes, and his name is Mac."

He ignored her comment as he picked the last plate out of the soapy water and rinsed it, then let the water run out of the sink. "Will the electricity stay on now? Do we have to take any precautions?"

Honey nodded. "A few. We still have to conserve electricity, and before bed I have to turn the generator off until tomorrow morning, but other than that, everything's fine." She wondered how a man could look so sexy when up to his elbows in dishwater. Life just wasn't fair. . . .

"You look beat," he said, coming up behind her as he wiped his hands dry on a dish towel.

"Thank you," she bit out. "A woman always likes to know when she's at her best."

A heavy sigh escaped him as he flung the towel onto the kitchen table. "I didn't mean it that way and you damn well know it." Then his hands rested a moment on her neck and shoulders before gently massaging the tension from her stiff muscles. At first touch she stiffened, but the more his hands moved on her skin, the more relaxed she became.

"Ummm," she moaned, closing her eyes and allowing her head to drop forward.

"You like?" His voice was low, soft, almost hypnotic. He reached under her mass of golden-brown hair to curl his fingers around the slender shaft of her neck, stroking the length of a knotted muscle.

"I love. You have gentle hands." She rolled her head from side to side to give him better access. Her eyes were closed, her breathing even.

He chuckled, his hands dropping back to her shoulder blades and working that area, kneading firmly but gently through her sweater. Suddenly his hand was gone, then she felt it slip inside her neckline moving a bra strap off her shoulder. She gave a faint gasp, but before she could protest, his hand was on the outside, kneading again. "Relax, Honey. I don't bite unless you're wearing a uniform."

"You and my German shepherd. But that doesn't mean neither of you is dangerous."

"You have a dog?"

"I had. Dexter died last year, and I haven't had the heart to replace him yet." Her once-taut muscles were beginning to feel like Jell-O, all loose and soft and so very warm.

"Meagan has always wanted a dog."

"Has she ever had one?"

"No," he said softly. "It's too hard to keep a dog in the city. I promised her that we'd move into the country sometime soon."

That statement surprised her. She looked over her shoulder at him. "You? Live in the country?" He might as well have said he was going to take up ranching. Either prospect was impossible for her to imagine. He just wasn't the country type!

"Turn around," he ordered, and without thought she obeyed. His hands continued their magic. "First of all," he began in a conversational tone, "you're right. I'm not a country boy. However, that doesn't mean I can't *live* in the country."

A little grunt emerged from her throat, and he knew it meant she doubted his opinion.

"Don't be so narrow-minded," he admonished, kneading a particularly sore spot and making her groan in reaction. "Surely you don't believe that everyone has one niche in life and they can't ever cross the line from one life-style to another, do you?"

"Actually, I do believe that. I couldn't live your life in the city any more than you could live mine in the country. There are fundamental differences in people that cannot be changed, and when they try to go against the very thing that makes them tick, they get caught in a way that always does them more harm than good." Her voice was thick, the words halting. His hands had made it almost too much of an effort to talk.

"Do you have a case in point?" Gradually his fingers worked toward her collarbone, the tips tracing the bone itself until they came into contact with the other bra strap. Once more his hand slid under the sweater neckline and slipped the strap aside.

Only this time she didn't react at all. His action seemed natural, and she never wanted his hands to stop their magic. She hadn't been so relaxed in days.

But she forced her brain to come up with an answer. "You and me, for instance."

His hands paused for a brief second before resuming their coaxing. Funny. Why did *coaxing* pop into her mind when the word should have been *kneading*?

"Honey?" His voice sounded far away and raspy, echoing through her body much as his touch was. "What about us?"

"We're . . ." She cleared her throat and started over, trying to focus on her thoughts instead of his hands...those wonderful magical hands. "Neither of us is suited to switching life-styles. You would wither in the country and I would simply dry up in the city."

"How do you know? Have you ever tried it?"

She stiffened at his question. "Yes," she said grimly. "And it was disaster."

"For whom?"

"Everyone involved."

"If more people thought like you, the West would never have been settled," he observed quietly.

She didn't protest or respond, just waited for him to go on. She expected him to try to persuade her to come over to his view.

When Beau said nothing more, she looked over her shoulder at him. His frown of concentration deepened as his fingers worked on her collarbone, the tips of his fingers barely caressing the beginning swell of her breasts. It didn't seem to bother him to touch her there, but that certainly wasn't her situation.

Suddenly she felt claustrophobic, and her hands covered his, halting his actions. "Thank you, Beau, but that's enough." She faced him, making sure she was just out of arm's reach. "I think I'll go take a hot shower."

"Fine." His expression was impassive, his eyes as cold as emeralds. "I'll be ready for one after you finish. Meagan could use a bath, too."

When he mentioned the child, Honey glanced around for the first time. She hadn't given a single thought to her since her father had begun his magic fingers act. "Where is she?"

Beau smiled. "In the living room watching her favorite program."

Honey's full mouth formed a silent O, and his eyes riveted to them, homing in like radar on a target. She could sense his invisible touch from across the room, and instead of fleeing she stood still, rooted to the floor as an intense wave of desire flooded through her.

"Do you have any wine?"

She nodded, but her eyes asked the silent question.

"Good," he said, finally turning away and allowing relief to soothe her. "We'll celebrate the electricity and the ability to bathe." A moment later he was gone from the room, walking down the hall toward the living room.

Honey expelled a sigh, feeling drained of every last shred of her energy. That man was far more potent in the same room than he was on TV. In the flesh he was downright lethal!

That's why she felt so drawn to him. It wasn't just her. All the women he encountered probably felt as she did in his presence or he wouldn't be the success he was. Therefore, it was all right to feel soft and mushy when he was around. But it certainly was *not* all right to follow the course those feelings were plotting for her!

Less than half an hour later, she had showered, washed and dried her hair, and had put on a touch of makeup. She scrutinized herself in the mirror, doubts flooding her. Nevertheless she smiled slowly in satisfaction. It wasn't a lot of makeup, just a hint of blusher and some mascara, no more than she usually wore when visiting clients. After three days of running around like a grubby cowhand, it felt good to be feminine again. She slipped a flame-colored caftan over her head. It was the only one she owned, and she loved it.

She called downstairs to let Beau know the bathroom was empty, then disappeared into her room until she heard him go in.

Quickly, with nerves once more tense and poised for action, she went downstairs and put wineglasses in the freezer to chill. She felt wild and daring and ready for anything. She felt desirable. She felt *womanly*. She just hoped Beau didn't think all her efforts were only for him. She needed this time just as much for herself as for her own self-esteem.

BEAU STOOD UNDER cold needles of water that stung his body. He hoped he wouldn't catch pneumonia. Cursing himself under his breath, he rubbed the bar of soap across the hair on his chest and under his arms.

That woman had really got to him, and he couldn't see how it had happened.

All right, so she was beautiful in a wholesome way, but he had never been attracted to women like that. She had a nice figure—a very nice figure, in fact—but so did thousands of other women.

But when she had walked into the kitchen after seeing that Mac character off, she had looked so vulnerable and so totally exhausted. He wondered how much he and Meagan had contributed to her tiredness.

At home there were always people coming and going, demanding this and that, and the telephone constantly rang. Parties were forever spilling forth like wine from a never-empty carafe.

While he didn't always like it, he was used to it.

But she wasn't. She seemed highly organized, a creature of habits that hardly ever varied, even to eating lunch and dinner at the same time every day. Why she wasn't bored to tears was beyond him. Even the view was the same, day in and day out: long expanses of pasture that, when there wasn't a storm flooding the land, he'd bet would vary only by the location of the grazing cattle.

He turned off the shower and stepped out, rubbing a towel briskly on his chest and arms. Looking down, he realized that although the cold shower had helped, it hadn't completely erased the effects of the erotic pictures of Honey his vivid imagination had created.

He groaned aloud. He had to stop all this if he was going to act normally around her instead of like a teenager.

Now to dress, then give Meagan a bath and ready her for bed.

He yawned. This country air was more restful than he'd thought. Suddenly he felt as tired as Honey had looked earlier. If he was lucky, the hurricane would blow itself out during the night and tomorrow's sun would dry up the deluge sufficiently so that he'd be able to leave.

He dressed quickly, then called Meagan. She came running, her sandals slapping the hardwood steps as she climbed the stairs one at a time.

His heart swelled again as he realized that his biggest prayer had been answered. He had his daughter back. Who needed anything else when, even on a disastrous day, the sunshine of her smile could make him feel ten feet tall again?

"Count your blessings, McGuire," he muttered as he swung her into his arms for a hug, then carried her back to the bathroom for Meagan's turn in the tub.

A father's work was never done.

It was nine o'clock by the time Beau finally ventured downstairs. He had tucked Meagan in and had read her favorite story to her, before she had dropped off to sleep. Outside the living room his feet halted, refusing to move another step.

Honey was sipping a glass of wine by the large bay window, a golden-red caftan swirling around her like the reflected glow from a bonfire. Her hair was loose, resting on her shoulders and framing her face delightfully. She seemed unreal, a vision of a fire goddess from some Nordic saga. When he stopped, she turned toward him, the brown of her eyes turning molten with heat and warmth and promises that singed his skin with wanting.

"Is Meagan asleep?" she asked huskily, and once more he became aware of her soft Southern accent rippling like dark rum through his body, seeping into places he didn't know wanted the sweetness of her.

"Yes," he answered, at last able to move toward the coffee table where a bottle of wine and a chilled glass waited for him.

"She's a wonderful child, Beau. You must be very proud."

"I am," he said but his attention was wholly on Honey. Standing so close to her, he couldn't even think clearly. Clearly? He could hardly think at all.

Honey gave a low chuckle. "And she looks just like you."

He poured the wine into his glass until it reached the brim, then took a large swallow of it. "She definitely looks like me, but Shelly deserves all the credit for her brightness. She's studying to be a teacher, and she practices on her. Meagan can write the entire alphabet and numbers up to ten."

Honey chuckled again, remembering the first night she had read to Meagan. Looking back, she wasn't sure it hadn't been the other way around. "I know what you mean."

The room grew silent for a moment. Something primordial was crackling in the air, charging the space with sheer electricity.

Honey walked over to the couch and sat down, cradling her wineglass in both hands. "You must have loved her mother very much," she said even before she realized it. One hand rose to cover her mouth, wishing those words away.

After his surprise, his green eyes showed he understood what she had really meant.

He sat beside her, leaning his head back and closing his eyes to rid himself of the image of Honey standing by the window. Torrid heat flowed through his veins at the memory. "I was twenty-seven when I met Pamela. I fell for her like the proverbial ton of bricks. But contrary to what most people believe, true opposites rarely stick together long enough to build a lasting relationship. Not opposites like we were, anyway." He sipped his wine, wondering why he was speaking of it now. He had never talked about that time before. Not to anyone.

"We were both trying to break into show business, but I had just auditioned for the part I'm playing now. When I got it, we were both ecstatic, but it also meant learning new lines and establishing a character every single day. Pamela loved to party, to spend money on clothes and things, to be constantly admired." He shrugged, hiding the hurt that surfaced within him. "I didn't have the time for that, and I certainly couldn't afford it."

"Was she beautiful?"

"Yes." He opened his eyes and looked at Honey. "As beautiful as you are tonight. But she was also shallow. She wanted everyone to *make* her happy instead of finding her own happiness."

Honey's heart went out to him for the misery he must have known. She touched her hand to his sleeve and gave his arm a light squeeze. "Don't feel sorry for me," he said huskily, reaching out a thumb to gently brush away the dampness on her lash.

She smiled. "I wasn't. I was feeling sorry for me."

"You?" She nodded, and he looked surprised. "Why?"

"Because my marriage followed the same pattern."

He opened his arms, and she came into their comfort, her head resting against his broad chest as if it belonged there. "Tell me about it."

She shook her head. "There's nothing much to tell. Peter was a beautiful man who thought that the world owed him happiness, no matter at whose expense."

"It's a wonder you didn't get a divorce."

"I—" She stopped, then cleared her throat and shook her head, unable to explain. She snuggled into the hollow of his neck, breathing deeply of the spicy scent of him.

"Honey, I . . ." He looked down at her, the words caught in his throat. The faint fragrance of strawberry shampoo mixed with the scent of her soap and her natural perfume assailed him.

"Yes?" She hadn't turned her head, but he could feel the heat from her body, the fire of her reaching out to turn him to honeyed liquid again.

"Let's make a toast," he said, unable to come up with anything else.

She raised her head, those dark brown eyes delving deeply into his. "To what?"

"To you, Meagan and me. To the storm for bringing us together." He lifted his glass to hers, the crystal tinkling musically.

"To us and the storm," she repeated gravely, her eyes following the movement of the glasses until they touched their lips. Her own mouth pursed sweetly, and he found himself shuddering as the liquid slid into her mouth, was savored on her tongue, then swallowed. Though he hadn't taken his own sip yet, he had swallowed with her.

Without a thought to what he was doing, he finished his wine, then took away her glass and set them both onto the table. Turning back to her, he saw a look in her eyes that told him whatever her fears had been, they wouldn't deter him. He needed her. Now. He had to have her arms around him, holding him as he was longing to hold her.

A kiss. One kiss. That was all. It was the only thought in his mind as he pulled her to him and lowered his head to cover her damp, slightly parted mouth with his.

Once his lips touched hers, he couldn't think at all.

6

HIS TOUCH TOOK HER BREATH AWAY, his kiss numbed her thoughts as she wrapped her arms around his neck to bring him closer. All her senses were heightened as a lightning bolt of warmth shot through her body. At first his hands explored her back, then one hand pressed her hips toward his while the other roamed from her back to her shoulder. Finally he crushed her to him, unwilling to allow any space between them, twining his fingers in the silken strands of her golden hair.

She was dazed. From far away she heard someone breathing heavily, and realized it was herself. His lips slipped away to travel down her cheek and pause on her slim neck, sipping her scent, tasting her special flavor as if she were the candy he had craved as a child. When one hand cupped a full breast, the breath caught in her throat, frozen. His thumb caressed its budding center, and it flowered instantly for him in gratitude.

When a low moan escaped her, he caught it with his mouth, his thumb pressing just a little harder as his palm circled her breast.

"Honey," he whispered hoarsely. "I want you."

She couldn't speak, couldn't utter the words he needed to hear. Instead, she nodded her head, craving even more than the intimate touch only he could give her. She had been alone for so very long. Being held by Beau brought back all the cravings she thought she had so successfully denied over the years.

But should she give into those feelings she had feared from her first look at him? One glimpse of his green eyes told her the answer. He really wanted her. He didn't want someone else nor to use her as a mere fill-in for another. *He wanted her!* And she wanted so desperately to be wanted.

"Yes," she murmured softly.

His eyes searched hers. "Are you sure?"

She smiled, suddenly feeling a soaring confidence. "Yes, Beau, I am."

Taking his hand, she led him to the stairs. He followed along quietly, almost obediently. They walked up the steps slowly, their tread barely audible above the droning rain. When she reached his door, he stopped her, tugging her back and wrapping her in his arms.

"Meagan's in my bed," he whispered in her ear.

She stiffened.

As if reading her mind, he stepped back and looked down at her in the dimness of the hallway. "I thought that might be easier on you in the morning."

Then his lips claimed her and wiped out all reason. When he lifted her to carry her into the bedroom, she made no protest. She couldn't. She didn't remember wanting anything as much as she wanted Beau at this moment.

He stopped by the side of the bed, standing her up to lean against him while he slid hungry hands over her, telling her with more than words just how desirable she was.

His fingers coaxed tingles from her swelling breasts, his mouth encouraged a duel from her lips, his hips were urgent against the concavity of hers. She answered him with soft, teasing strokes of her own. She taunted his earlobes with light fingertips, then followed the curl and curve of his ears before resting her palms against his jaw, feeling the slight abrasiveness of his freshly shaved cheek. It felt so good. So masculine.

When his hand settled around her neck, he found her zipper and slowly pulled it down. She shivered, not from the chill of the night air, but from the blazing touch of his fingers. Her caftan floated over her breasts and hips to circle her feet.

Her own fingers were busy, too. They trembled as they unbuttoned the shirt that followed his body contours so well. She hesitated when she reached the snap of his cords, uncertain for the first time.

"Please, don't stop now," he groaned.

Her eyes darted to his face, seeing the tautness there, and her hands shook all the more.

Until she heard the snap release, she held her breath, then let it out in a sigh that caressed his bare chest with its warmth, forcing his hand to tighten his hold on her throbbing breast. His zipper was far easier.

Suddenly their mouths were meeting again, his tongue invading her, thanking, soothing her for her earlier efforts, and she melted against him. The confusion, the indecision, fled, and in its place was a fever of desire that seemed to spiral high and higher. Tendrils of a deep-seated urgency twined through her, knotting her insides and tightening further the constant pressure created by the feel of his body against hers.

"Your touch," he grated into her ear when he finally pulled away.

"My touch?" she asked, her voice almost a whisper.

"It's so sweet. Like honey. Like you." His lips sought the hollow of her throat before he bent farther and laved her rigid nipple with his tongue. She soothed him with her palms, trailing her fingertips across his shoulders and back, losing them in the nape of his neck, testing the softness of his midnight-dark hair.

"More," she whispered.

He obliged her, and drew a response right down to the tips of her toes. She felt limp with passion, and from the dim recesses of her mind a voice told her she had never felt this way before. Not even the best times in the past had been so wonderful. But her thoughts wouldn't merge to form the words; only the feelings were present. She was too hungry with desire for Beau to do anything but obey his slightest wish. Anything he wanted he could have, as long as he gave her sustenance—her reward for feeling this way.

He pulled away from her, his hands clasped in hers, drawing her onto the quilted spread. His green eyes gleamed as he watched her body slide up the side of the bed to make room for him. God, she was beautiful. So very genuine. His eyes widened at that thought, wondering briefly where it had come from. Only three days ago he had thought her plain because she wore men's clothes and her face was unpainted. Now he was simply pleased. Beneath those men's clothes was a beautiful woman's body, curved and soft, warm and responsive to his every touch. He felt ten feet tall.

Her hands stretched out to him imploringly, and he obeyed at once, slipping his cords down. He was beside her almost instantly, his hands traveling satin-pink skin, stroking the silkiness of her stomach and thighs. She melted even more, silently encouraging him by acquiescing to his every wish, and that willingness made him heady with the wonder of it all.

When he entered her, they both sighed, then held their breaths as the rhythm of love began its own drumbeat in their heads.

Honey closed her eyes and savored the presence of Beau rising above her. It had been so long since anything had felt this right. So long . . .

With each thrust his name burned deeper into her soul. Beau, Beau, Beau.

And then came the soaring mountain peak. The near-silent whistling of wind and the searing caress of their heat filled her whole being. For the tiniest moment she was still, then her grip tightened on his shoulders as she felt him pulse deeply within her.

"Beautiful. So beautiful," he said raggedly against her cheek. Then a scant moment later he fell asleep. Two moments later, Honey was asleep, too. Her head was against his chest, her lips curled in a small smile that she never knew was there.

When gray dawn crept through the curtains, Honey snuggled instinctively against Beau. His arm tightened, drawing her even closer, and before she knew it she was instigating more lovemaking. Now it was her turn to lead, to show him how to follow. It was her turn to grasp the reins and guide them up the mountain peak. And she did.

COFFEE-SCENTED AIR filled the kitchen. Cereal, butter and jam were already on the table, which was set for breakfast. When Beau and Meagan came down, Honey would start breakfast.

While she waited she looked out the kitchen window, watching the rain coming down. The storm had let up a lot since last night. The weather had changed, and all the signs of the hurricane's demise were visible. The floodwaters would gradually recede, and then would come the cleanup of downed power lines and other debris.

Yesterday she had noticed that one large oak on the back of her property had been uprooted, but that appeared to be all the damage the storm had done. She'd been one of the lucky ones and she prayed that her neighbors could say the same. The storm could have taken off some roofs, splintered trees onto homes, done any amount of damage....

Last night there had been a different kind of storm inside her house. In her bedroom. Inside her. Her nerves tingled at the very thought of it.

She had been married for three years and widowed for three more, and last night was as far outside her normal experience as the past few years had been routine. Her marriage with Peter had in no way prepared her for the intense storm of emotions she had felt last night with Beau.

Now what was she going to do? To say? Without her telling him, Beau wouldn't know that she had never known anything like their loving last night. Ever. And she certainly wouldn't tell him!

As she brought her coffee cup to her lips, her hands shook with the effort.

She was so confused! One part of her insisted that she had wanted Beau's lovemaking last night, that she needed to be held and touched and made love to so tenderly that remembering it brought tears to her eyes. She had needed to know she was a desirable woman.

But another part of her told her that she might never recuperate from the desolation of his departure.

And that thought hurt too much to bear considering.

"Good morning." Beau's voice sounded like a low, possessive growl as his arms slid around to the front of her, resting lightly on the slight swell of her belly.

"Good morning." She made no move to turn around and confront him. Not yet.

"Mmmm, you smell better than the coffee." He nuzzled her neck, his clean-shaven jaw tickling slightly.

"And you've already shaved." His intimate closeness was capturing her breath.

"I thought it was the least I could do. Otherwise you might not allow me to greet you the way I wanted to."

Honey gulped, then placed her cup carefully on the counter. "Is Meagan awake yet?"

"No, the little sleepyhead is still cuddling her bunny." His voice held that special note of tenderness he reserved for his daughter.

"Would you like some coffee?" If her nerves had been troubled before, what in heaven's name were they doing now? Getting ready to shatter?

"Not as much as I'd like to carry you back up those stairs and into your room," he murmured in her ear before turning her around to pull her head against his bare chest. Involuntarily her arms slid around his waist, her thumbs looping into the waistband of his cords as she rested her cheek against his rumbling heartbeat.

He smelled good—so clean and so completely male. It was all she could do to keep her hands from absorbing the strength of him as they wandered across his back. "The memories of last night have played through my head all morning, teasing me with some unusual ideas. I want to make love with you in as many different ways as we can invent."

"So what's keeping you?" she asked lightly.

As if in answer, his stomach growled, and they both chuckled. "Well, for one thing I'm starving, and I heard somewhere that man cannot live on love alone."

Her heart turned over at the word. Did he really mean love, or just lovemaking? If Honey had learned anything, it was the immense difference between those two words.

She forced a smile before looking up into the warmth of his eyes. "In that case, I'd better start breakfast. This is no time to have a weakened man on my hands," she said as she slipped out of his arms and moved toward the refrigerator. Bacon and eggs would keep her busy enough so she wouldn't be constantly reminded of the delicious taste of his lips or cozy feel of his embrace.

"Honey?"

At the sound of his voice, she glanced over her shoulder, noting the quick crease of a frown on his forehead. She lifted her brows in silent question.

"Are you upset this morning?"

She turned back to the refrigerator meat drawer, pulling out the bacon. "No, should I be?"

"No. But you're . . ." He stopped, waiting for the right words to form so he could explain himself.

"Distant? Cool?" she finally said, knowing instinctively what he meant and unable to play games with him.

"Yes." A flicker of surprise crossed his face before his eyes narrowed. His examination was all too thorough. "Are you? Is that how you really feel?"

She shook head, clutching the bacon, which was wrapped with the butcher paper, in her hands as she faced him. "No," she confessed. "Awkward might be a better word."

"Why?"

She shrugged. "Probably because I've never woken up in the morning and discovered a strange man in my bed. I'm not sure how I should act."

"And I wasn't supposed to figure that out?"

"I don't know."

"Honey, put down that damned bacon and listen to me," he ordered quietly. She put the package on the counter and turned to face him, her hands clasped loosely before her.

For a moment he just stood there, his eyes distracted by the droplets of rain on the window as he groped for reassuring words. "I don't quite know how last night evolved, but I do know I'm not sorry. I loved making love with you last night and I would love to make love to you again tonight. But I'm not going to force you into anything. I'm not even going to ask. This has got to be a two-way street, Honey. You've got to want me, too, or it doesn't work."

"I know," she whispered. "It's just that it's all so new to me."

His features softened. "You're very special, do you know that?"

"How?" Her eyes widened.

"For one thing, you're so direct. You come right out and say what's on your mind."

"And you like that?"

He chuckled wryly. "I don't know whether I do or not, but I am fascinated by it. I've never known anyone who was so honest with me."

A tremor of pain crossed her face. "Well, I've never known many honest people, either. So I guess we're even." Her voice held just a hint of bitterness, but it was enough to draw him to within inches of her. Love had always been part of a package deal, she thought to herself. I'll love you if you do this for me, or if you promise me that. Her parents, her husband, they had all put some kind of price tag on love.

His hands gently held the sides of her face as he tilted her mouth toward his without touching it. "Maybe we're good for each other, restoring a little faith in the opposite sex. Who knows?" His smile was slow and easy, and she responded to it like budding flowers to spring sunshine. His lips quickly brushed hers, light but branding in their power. "And now, if you don't mind, I'm starving. You cook and I'll clean."

And she did.

By the time Honey finished making breakfast, Meagan was up. They all sat down to a table laden with the goodies, right down to freshly baked biscuits.

He must have enjoyed the food because Beau filled his plate twice. Meagan chattered away, oblivious to the thin strand of nonverbal communication that connected Honey and Beau.

"Rain's letting up," Beau mentioned at one point.

"It will likely rain off and on for the next day or two, but the wind will die down," Honey predicted. "The main storm is over."

It seemed as if they had been on a remote island, cut off from the world, but soon it would intrude, and Honey could feel the imminence of a kind of sadness, too.

"How long does it usually take for the creeks to go down?"

"Only a day or two. Houston and Harris County are mostly sand right about sea level. The water that can't be absorbed has to run off."

"So it really won't be safe to drive to Austin or Houston for a few more days?" Beau asked as he busily buttered another biscuit. Honey could have sworn he was pleased with the fact.

"Right," she said as she began clearing the table. Meagan scooted off her chair and carefully carried her plate to the counter. Honey couldn't help the feeling of pride that washed over her as she watched the little girl. She bent down and gave the child a hug, and Meagan hugged back, giggling.

"Do you want to come and help me with the chores?" she asked. Meagan nodded and scampered off to find her jacket.

Honey turned to find Beau watching her with rapt attention. "I've never seen Meagan take to anyone like she has to you. Not even her Aunt Shelly gets that positive a response."

"She's a darling," Honey said, for once hiding behind an inane comment. How could she tell him that in his child Honey had found a kindred soul? It didn't even make sense to her.

"Yes, she is," Beau agreed, but his mind seemed to be elsewhere.

He went along with them to the barn, stepping carefully around the larger puddles. Meagan and Honey laughed, sloshing through in the big rubber boots that protected them from the worst of the mud.

He helped her shove open the heavy barn doors, realizing just how good her muscle tone was. The doors were large and cumbersome, and she moved them every day.

He watched her climb the ladder to the loft, then call out a warning as she threw down a bale of hay. After she came down and started pitching it around, he began to feel more and more useless by the moment.

"Do you have another pitchfork? I'll help," he offered.

"No thanks. Just make sure Meagan doesn't get too close to momma cat or that she doesn't try to hug a guinea hen. They're just a little on the independent side." She never slowed the rhythm of her movements, and Beau stood awkwardly on the sidelines, hands in his pockets.

"Don't touch, Meagan," Honey admonished softly as she began pouring water into the cat's bowl a few minutes later. "Here, put this food in the other bowl for me. Okay?" She handed the child a small dented pan with cat food in it.

Meagan carefully stooped, pouring cat food, grain by grain, into the dish. Honey couldn't help smiling. Her amusement was noted by Beau, leaning against the rough planks of a empty horse stall. He looked positively forlorn.

"Beau, could you reach behind you and grab that shovel? The side stall over here needs mucking out."

"Mucking out?"

She smiled. "You fork up the straw and manure and toss it into that wheelbarrow." She gestured toward the corner where a rusty wheelbarrow sat.

"Great," he muttered under his breath.

"It's a dirty job, but someone has to do it," she said, chuckling.

While Beau "mucked," Honey scattered fresh hay. Unconsciously Beau was making a face, almost closing up his nostrils so the pungent odor wouldn't invade his lungs. But when Honey leaned on her pitchfork, laughing so hard she couldn't seem to control herself, it dawned on him that he was the target of her laughter. Not until he noticed Meagan was laughing, too, did he relax enough to see the humor of it all.

"So, I'm that funny looking, huh?" he teased, dropping to his haunches in front of Meagan and allowing a hint of his smile to show.

"Uh-huh," she giggled, her green eyes bright with laughter. "You looked like a guinea hen, Daddy, with your nose up!"

Honey stood nearby, a smile lingering on her lips as she watched father and daughter give each other a hug. When they stood up, Meagan slipped her hand into his.

"What's the matter?" Beau asked, his green eyes searching Honey's now drooping smile. "Are you feeling all right?"

She smiled again, but this time it was forced. "I'm fine," she said brightly. "And nearly finished." With more industriousness than she had shown all day, she quickly completed the regular chores.

"Ready?" she asked.

"Ready," Meagan and Beau chorused. Then Beau stiffened, holding Meagan back from the entrance to the barn. "Everybody stay still," he ordered in a voice harsh with command.

Startled, Honey turned toward him. He was staring at the ground, and her gaze followed his.

Slowly Beau bent down and picked Meagan up, holding her in his arms as he began stepping away backward from the door.

"What's the..." Then she saw it. A greenish-brown snake was curled up near the door, its head raised and seeking air.

Honey started laughing, tears filling her eyes as she stared at the snake, then at Beau clutching Meagan as he stood rigidly against the stall door.

"What's so damn funny!" he roared, his frustration all too obvious.

"It's a—" she began, only to be forced to stop for breath. "It's a garden snake. It's harmless," she finally got out.

"A . . . Well, how in the world am I supposed to know that!" he bellowed.

"I'm sorry, Beau," she gasped, clutching his arm as she tried to quell the laughter and apologize at the same time. "I know it seems strange to you, but I've grown up with them all my life. I used to wear them around my neck like beads when I was a kid."

"Lady, you're crazy!" he said, edging his way past the snake and toward the house, muttering under his breath all the way.

She followed him out of the barn, carefully closing the doors before dodging puddles across the yard, all the time trying to control her grin.

An hour later he was sheepish, finally seeing the humor of the situation through Honey's eyes. She told him about the various snakes in the area and tried to educate him in some of the ways of the country.

At least she had managed to smooth his feathers some, for he had reached the point where he could chuckle now, too. Her estimation of him skyrocketed when he asked her questions that were direct and to the point, demonstrating just how much of her lesson had been absorbed.

Not until late afternoon did Meagan go for her nap. Beau vented a small sigh of relief, because at last he was alone with Honey. His hands were itching to touch her again; his lips felt as if they were in a perpetual pucker to kiss her. He hadn't felt so frustrated since high school when some girl had promised him a "good time." Except there was more to this feeling than mere anticipation. Much more.

Honey sat at her desk across the room. He could practically see the barriers she had erected during the day. He couldn't understand them. He wasn't sure how to go about it, but he knew that he had to tear them down. He patted the couch cushion next to his. "Come sit over here and leave those papers for a while. If you keep it up, you're going to shuffle them into confetti."

She looked up and gave a smile in his direction, but it never reached her eyes. "I'll be there in a minute. Just let me finish straightening up a bit."

"You finished that job twenty minutes ago," he pointed out. "Now come over here and let me hold you." The demanding expression in his eyes clearly warned her that if she didn't, he'd come to her. He watched her move slowly across the room, her gaze locked on the cushion next to him. When she sat down, her body was tense.

He tucked an arm around her shoulder, gently pulling her head against his chest, twining his fingers in her thick golden hair. Then he leaned back, realizing full well he was going to have to take it step by step. He expelled an exaggerated sigh.

"What's that for?" Honey asked, keeping her head averted to escape the unplumbed depths of his piercing green eyes.

"That's for contentment. I've been dying to hold you all day." He leaned back and closed his eyes just in case she looked up. He wanted her to feel relaxed. He *didn't* want her to know that he was straining at the bit to kiss her, to savor the softness of her flesh beneath his lips and hands.

Slowly he felt Honey let go. Her head snuggled against him, one hand resting easily on his thigh. It took all his willpower not to urge it farther up and to feel the heat of her against him. When he could finally speak, his voice was like a gentle caress. "Why do you lead such an isolated life, Honey?"

"I like it this way." He felt her body stiffen slightly, but at least she wasn't pulling away.

"Tell me about you," he said, his hand rising to gently stroke her arm, soothing away her tension.

"There's nothing much to tell." Her voice was muffled against his shirt.

"Did you ever want children? Were you happy? Did you love your husband? You said your marriage was like my relationship with Pamela. How?" His inquisition actually sounded polite, pitched almost too low for her to hear. But she tensed just the same. He praised heaven that she didn't leap from his arms.

"I thought I loved him," she said with hesitation, answering his last question first. "But I was wrong. We had nothing in common where it really counted. We met in college, fell in love and married. I moved into his apartment and went to work for an insurance company downtown. The only thing I did well was my job. I hated the city, the noise, the people. Everything."

Beau held his breath, imagining her as she was before her husband had come along. "When I met Peter," she continued, "he swept me off my feet with his good looks, his dazzle and his sophistication. It wasn't until later that I realized awe wasn't the same as love."

"And?" he prompted gently, kissing the top of her head and reveling in the wonderful scent of her hair.

"And he thought I was nice and sweet, and that was a change for him. But it was no basis for a marriage." She paused, wondering why she was volunteering her memories when she never had before. "We tried so hard to work out our differences. But neither of us appreciated the other's life-style or dreams. I wanted to be a wife and mother, and he wanted us to be involved in the bustle of Houston, doing the things he had always dreamed of—partying with important people, dancing and being seen at all the 'in' spots...."

She sighed. When she finally got the nerve to peep at Beau from beneath her lashes, she was surprised. His eyes were closed, his features utterly relaxed. His manner made it easier to go on. "Country girls are notorious for being self-sufficient loners, you know."

He chuckled, indicating he believed her. His hand squeezed her arm, encouraging her. He wasn't about to interrupt her by telling her that there were loners in the city, too.

"Well, we continued to try. Toward the end, he moved back to the country with me, but I knew he hated it here. He was a people person, and neither of us was adult enough or smart enough to find a solution to our dilemma."

"Then what happened?" His voice was almost a whisper.

"Then, surprise of surprises, he fell in love. With a girl from his past, whom he had gone with in high school." She swallowed and closed her eyes before she continued. The wounded pride was still intact and obvious, but the hurt was gone at last. Time had managed to heal the pain. "In some ways, it seems like yesterday that he came in here, sat me down and tried to explain his deep, abiding, love for another woman. A woman who'd had a place in his heart before he had ever met me."

Beau's arm tightened protectively, and she felt his comfort flow right through her to the core. "They had so much in common, you see," she said calmly, "and we had nothing left but the few early sparks of love. I asked him to give us another month, and eventually Peter agreed. A week later he was killed in an accident." Her hand tightened on Beau's thigh, and he held his breath for fear of halting her flow of words.

"Even after he was dead, I didn't really believe it. Almost every night I would wait for his Corvette to come up the driveway, spraying gravel. But he never came home again."

The lump in her throat kept her from speaking. Beau's hands pulled her closer as he felt her tremble. Curses formed in his brain at the gods who wreaked such capricious damage on so many innocents.

Her hand squeezed even tighter on his thigh, and he held her even closer. His lips grazed her temple, then he lifted her hand off his thigh to press a kiss into the center of her palm. He placed her hand on his chest where it would cause less damage to his libido while he waited for her to tell him the rest.

But when she remained silent, he was forced to prompt her. "What did you do then?"

"Nothing," Honey said. "I pretended it hadn't happened at all. I shoved everything to the back of my mind until much later." Her voice cracked, and she cleared her throat. "We all have to deal with things, though, sooner or later, whether we want to or not. It was that way for me, too."

"You know you can't carry all the blame, Honey. Whatever happened, it took both of you to create the circumstances." He caressed her hair as she leaned against him. Tears ran down her cheeks, dampening his shirt, but Beau didn't care. He cradled her, twisting her around so she was on his lap as he rocked back and forth, stroking her hair. Parallels. Pamela and

Peter had a lot in common. They both had left deep and abiding scars. . . .

"That's it, Honey, let it all out," he crooned, using her name as an endearment. She wrapped her arms around his neck, hiding her face against his shoulder.

"I'm sorry," she said eventually. She wiped her nose and eyes with the linen handkerchief he gave her, then laid her head back on his shoulder.

"I'm glad I was here," he replied, meaning every word. He knew Honey had got under his skin as no woman ever had, and he didn't care. It didn't matter that this was the closest he had come to any woman, including Pamela. There was something soft and vulnerable about this wonderfully self-sufficient woman, something that called out to him in a hundred ways.

He could see Honey so clearly as the person she really was, but looking back he realized that, with Pamela, he had never allowed himself to see the woman she was, teetering up there on the pedestal he had erected for her. He thought he had gone into their relationship with his eyes open, but he realized now he had never been able to see what was right in front of him. Just like Honey, he had been attracted first and then had dreamed of the person he had wanted Pamela to be instead of looking at her as she really was. He'd been as much at fault with her as Honey had been with her Peter. . . .

They were two fools who had got burned when they had mistaken lust for love instead of taking the time to look for the real thing.

Well, the past was gone. It wasn't important anymore. What was important slept in the upstairs bedroom and relaxed contentedly in his arms.

That thought shocked the hell out of him.

He looked down at Honey. What did he feel for her? Love? Impossible. Hell, he'd only know her for three days and had made love to her one night. He didn't need to be an accountant to know that it didn't add up to a commitment. That made it a toss in the hay.

Don't kid yourself, McGuire, a little voice in his head said, and he knew it was right. Regardless of the time, this woman had stirred him deeply the moment he'd entered her home.

Honey stirred in his arms. "Thanks, Beau, for listening." She wriggled as if to sit up. In response, he tightened his arms and pulled her close to his chest again.

"You're not going anywhere, so just lean back and enjoy it," he teased as his hands began straying lightly but with obvious intent over her body. He had been waiting all day to touch her, and he wasn't about to lose the chance now. His palm curled to her breast like a petal to the heart of a new rose. A sigh escaped from her lips, and her breath warmed the hollow his throat.

"Mmmm." She covered his hand with hers and pressed it more intimately against her.

She tilted her head toward his, and his lips claimed hers in a kiss that spoke of passion and tenderness and new, tumultuous emotions neither was willing nor ready to label yet. Her arms wrapped around his neck, pressing her body against the hardness of his in an unspoken plea. He obeyed at once, his hand moving deftly up her jean-clad thigh to rest at the juncture of her legs. The radiant warmth of her wrapped him in a blanket from which no escape was wanted or possible.

His tongue dueled hers for supremacy before giving in to stroke the softness of her mouth in entreaty. They both knew what they wanted but neither chose to voice it. Instead, hands and tongues and bodies did the asking and the answering.

Tears still dampened her cheeks to remind him of the tragedies of her life, and he felt his heart skip a beat. He wanted to soothe, to love, to protect her. To take care of her.

He wanted her.

"I need you, Honey," he murmured against her creamy skin. "Now." She grew still in his arms.

"Look at me," he urged.

Her luminous brown eyes, shot with gold, gazed at him. He could lose himself in those eyes.

"Say it, Honey. Say you want me, too. Say you need me with you, making love with you. Sheathed deep inside you." His words were soft, but his eyes were relentless.

She only hesitated a moment, but in that silent time an alien noise filtered into their cocoon.

Meagan was awake from her nap.

A groan erupted deep in his chest even as good humor sparkled in Honey's eyes. Their needs would have to wait a little while longer.

7

IF EVER BEAU HAD KNOWN utter frustration, it was nothing compared to this.

"I'd better check on what we'll have for dinner." A smile still delightfully tilted her lips upward, showing her dimple.

"And I'd better head for a cold shower," he grumbled ungraciously. "I obviously need to think of something else."

"You mean other than how to fill a rainy afternoon?" Her voice was teasing, her brown eyes still dancing with mirth.

"Exactly."

"You could always play paper dolls." She offered the suggestion while standing in the living room doorway so she could think more clearly. When he was close, her system went haywire.

"The only doll I want to play with isn't made of paper," Beau pointed out, the smoky gleam in his turbulent eyes underlining his frustration.

Honey chuckled, then waved bye-bye. As she turned to walk to the kitchen, Meagan hopped off the bottom step.

"Hello, punkin', " Honey said, a smile still in her voice.

"Is Daddy here?" Meagan's little forehead was creased in a sleepy frown.

"He's in the living room, sweetheart. Waiting for you." Honey bent down and kissed the top of the little girl's head. "I'm going to see what we have for dinner."

"Popsicles?"

"Not tonight, Meagan. Maybe later," she said, feeling a comfortable wash of contentment. She was in love all right. Better, she had the completeness of a family tucked around her. Everything was right with her world. Today. She refused to consider tomorrow or the next day. That would come soon enough.

Sometime later Honey stood stirring simmering spaghetti sauce on the back of the old wood stove. The generator was working fine, but she didn't want to overload it with her high-voltage electric range. Keeping busy, she had cleaned out the pantry and checked on the frozen food in the refrigerator and the freezer.

And Beau sat at the kitchen table, one big ache. His mind was consumed with the prospect of holding Honey again. Meagan had to call him three times before her voice registered.

"Daddy! What you doing?" she asked, obviously exasperated with him. The little girl had been kneading the fresh bread dough Honey had made. Not until he looked down did he realize he'd been pulling on the white cloth used for shielding the table as Meagan worked.

"Sorry, sweetheart," he said, finally moving himself out of the room and away from the source of his frustration. He walked upstairs to his room and stood at the window, glaring at the drizzle and wet ground below.

He knew there was a road out there somewhere, but right now nothing could be seen, not even another house. The whole area looked like a giant one-inch-deep lake. He could have been on a thousand acres in the middle of the wilderness instead of on ten acres just outside Houston, the fifth largest city in the United States.

Beau turned his back on the scene. Isolation. Total isolation. He, Meagan, Honey. He said it aloud. "Beau, Meagan, and Honey." It sounded good. Too damn good. He lay on the bed, hands cupped behind his head, and sifted through his jumbled emotions, trying to create some kind of order.

BY THE TIME the water began heating for the spaghetti, Honey's nerves were stretched to a breaking point. Her thoughts raced helter-skelter, probing every niche of her body seeking clarity. She had glanced over her shoulder toward the kitchen door more times than she could count, waiting for Beau to return. When had she ever done that before? Never.

Not even with Peter, who was now only a dim memory.

This afternoon in the living room, Beau's sympathy and understanding had encouraged her to reach a true catharsis. She had only broken down once before, and that had been two years ago when she had glanced at the calendar and realized it was the anniversary of Peter's death.

She checked the doorway again, unconsciously seeking the object of her thoughts. Realization spilled over her. These feelings she had for Beau were exactly what she had been fighting against these past days. But she couldn't deny the attraction any longer.

It was all she could do to wait for nightfall and Meagan's bedtime. She guiltily glanced at the little girl industriously patting the dough on the table. She was a darling. A feminine carbon copy of her father. No wonder he treasured her so.

"Momma?" Meagan's voice was high and wavering, and as Honey turned around again, she saw a large crystal tear threatening to dampen the child's cheek.

She stepped quickly to Meagan's side. "What is it, darlin'? What's the matter?"

"My bread popped at me," Meagan explained in a soft voice, her bottom lip quivering, her feelings obviously hurt.

Honey's brow creased as she stared at the offending dough on the table, an air hole marring the smooth, floured surface. "The bread popped?" She looked at the dough, then at Meagan, for the first time noticing that her nose was covered with a dusting of flour. Then she grinned. While kneading, Meagan must have created an air hole and then hit it with her hand, forcing a small geyser of flour into the air.

Honey, half laughing, tried to erase the little girl's woebegone look. "It didn't mean to, punkin'. It's just the nature of the beast," she said, enveloping Meagan in a hug. "Don't pay any attention to it. We need to get it into the oven now, anyway."

Her voice was reassurance enough that Meagan hadn't done anything wrong. Her green eyes began to sparkle again, the lower lip settling down enough to turn up in the beginning of a smile.

"I'll tell you what, Meagan," Honey began. "We'll put this in the oven, then go tell your dad just what happened. Okay?"

At Meagan's energetic nod, Honey grabbed the bread pan from the counter and prepared it for the oven. She couldn't get the dough in it fast enough to suit her, her mind was so preoccupied with Beau. Deftly she set the timer to warn her when the bread was ready, then she was out of the kitchen, Meagan's hand tightly in hers, in search of Beau.

"Beau?" Her voice was light as air.

"In here," he called through the partially opened guest room door. Honey smiled down at Meagan. As she pushed the door open all the way and stared across the room, her heart was in her throat.

Beau was reclining on the bed, his hands behind his head, enjoying her movement as she walked across the room toward his.

She swallowed hard. The muscles in his arms stretched the material of his shirtsleeves, his broad chest and slim hips emphasized all the more by his position. But it was his eyes that were the most riveting. Their deep forest green turned her flesh to molten lava as they hinted of delights to come when Meagan was asleep and the house was surrounded by darkness.

Beau swung his legs off the side of the bed and opened his arms to Meagan. But his eyes never left Honey's face except to caress the length of her body as if to remind himself that he hadn't been dreaming of her lushness. A warmth suffused her, and her eyes slid to the floor, avoiding his all too clear messages.

Meagan sailed into Beau's open arms, her little bow mouth upturned in a giggle as she told her father the story of the burping bread dough. He laughed at the appropriate times, stroked her cap of curls and smiled when she gave him a kiss before skipping off to watch her favorite TV program.

The room echoed with the silence she had left behind.

"I missed you," he said simply.

She clutched the doorknob tighter. "Then why didn't you come downstairs?"

"Because I couldn't touch you downstairs," he stated calmly, rising slowly from the edge of the bed and walking toward her. "Ever since I met you, I've wanted to do the most impossible things to you," he teased. His hands encircled her waist, then trailed down to her hips to pull her closer. "That desire comes over me at the strangest times—in the kitchen, in the hallway, but especially when you sweep the floor and your little tush swings in that eye-catching way."

His lips touched her forehead, drifting down the line of her cheek to trail kisses to the corner of her mouth. "See what I mean?" he murmured against her parted mouth, his tongue barely teasing the soft flesh inside her lips.

"I see," she whispered, both arms circling his neck as she came even closer to him.

His mouth captured hers, his tongue mating and his hands blazing a path across her back and hips as he tried to totally envelop her. She found herself reeling from his touch, his kisses, reveling in the vibrant feelings overwhelming her, yet secretly she was frightened to death to admit it, even to herself.

"Honey." His deep voice was calloused. "So sweet, so soft."

She buried her cheek in the curve of his neck. "You aren't," she said breathlessly. "You're all hard angles and soft bumps." Her breath skimmed the flesh of his throat and sent a shiver of excitement through him.

"Bumps?" he finally managed, barely able to curb his need of her.

"Uh-huh," she murmured against his collarbone. "You know, like those new foam pillows. Firm underneath, with just a little give on the surface."

His chuckle rumbled in his chest. "I'll show you firm. Tonight."

"Promises, promises." She sighed, her lips opening just enough to nip his flesh, something she had never done before in her life. His passionate reaction was so immediate she was filled with power.

She looked up, her eyes so bright with love he could almost feel it. "I want to thank you for listening to my tale of woe this afternoon. I've never spoken about my marriage before. Suddenly I feel better than I have in years."

He smiled tenderly. "You're quite welcome. It goes both ways, you know. I've never really talked to anyone about Pamela." He kissed the tip of her upturned nose. "You helped me, lady. It was only fair that I return the favor."

The timer buzzed dimly from the kitchen, cutting off the moment. With a silent hug, she ducked out of his arms.

Beau leaned his forehead against the door frame. Things were moving entirely too fast. Three days ago he had shown up on her doorstep, and last night he'd made love to her as if she were the only oasis in the desert.

Where was this all leading? How could it be happening to him, a man who knew the rules of the game and had played it accordingly until now? He had thought he was beyond the feelings Honey had unleashed in him. He was sure his maturity and his bad experience with Pamela would have protected him from all this. He was wrong.

He couldn't understand a damn bit of it, and that made it more frustrating. Hell, Honey was so naive she probably wouldn't survive half the brittle, catty parties he had had to go to. The drawing-room politics that made or broke men and women in his business were based on mean-spirited deception and finagling, not on the basic human honesty that was so much a part of Honey. Until this second, he hadn't realized how much he had hated to play the games.

No, Honey would never make it in the city. She would wither and die if her cats, cows and chickens weren't around. He suspected she didn't know the first thing about survival in that big world out there....

Dinner that evening was a quiet affair. Although Meagan occasionally recounted one of Big Bird's stories of the day, when she finished, an easy silence returned.

After dinner, they watched TV, Meagan sprawled on the floor while Beau sat in the large wingback chair. Honey took the couch, going through a client's books and double-checking her figures.

She didn't look up until she heard Beau.

"Okay, Meagan. Say good-night to Honey. It's time for bed."

Meagan charged over to plant a wet kiss on Honey and deliver a bone-bruising hug. Honey kissed back, loving the feel of hugging the tiny body. When the hug and the kiss were over, Meagan was satisfied and ran back into her daddy's arms. Beau picked her up and carried her upstairs, talking to her in a low voice.

Meagan's giggles floated back down into the living room after echoing in the hallway. Honey's smile became a frown.

In a few days Meagan and Beau would be gone, and she'd be back to rattling around in this empty house again. But wasn't that what she wanted—her life to return to normal? Oh, Beau's lovemaking last night had been something to remember for always, and Meagan's darling company had been terrific, but she had only lived with them for three days; she had been alone for three years.

With trembling fingertips, she massaged her temples. There was no doubt about it. Beau and Meagan McGuire had stepped into her life, and everything about it had changed as a result. She just couldn't define what the meaning of the change was, or figure out if it was for better or worse.

Beau came down the stairs as quietly as he could, knowing Meagan would wake from her light sleep if she knew he had left. As he paused on the last step, staring into the living room at Honey, his heart swelled. How could he ever have thought she was plain? He had been incredibly naive to think it would be easy to come to Texas, pick up his daughter and beat a quick path back to New York without leaving a small part of him behind.

He watched the nervous way her fingers moved over her forehead and wondered if she was as upset as he. There was no way they could build a relationship, since anything between them had to end when he left. They just wouldn't fit into each other's worlds, no matter how strong the emotions were that tugged at them. Together, their lives were just as different as those of the people they had each both loved before, and possibly just as destructive to each other.

He clenched his hands at his sides. He knew and she knew, but somehow his emotions weren't getting the message. What he wanted most at this instant was to carry her back up those stairs and take her to bed, pressing every inch of her flesh into his until he absorbed her and sated himself.

Before he realized it, he was at her side, seated and gathering her into his arms. He sighed, his eyes closing at the sudden warm feeling of completeness that swept over him. His hands moved slowly over her back, seeking out the soft, firm skin. At once the tension that had been growing in him all day dissipated. He was content. Later he would make some hard decisions, but at the moment he needed to hold her, to feel her pliant in his arms, to reach out and touch her soul, as she had touched his.

"Beau?" Honey murmured against the curve of his shoulder.

"Hmmm?" He fingered the silken strands of honey-blond hair that were clinging to his shirt.

"Why? Why this? Now?"

His hand stilled. "I don't know." He sounded as confused as she felt. "I don't understand it. All I know for sure is that it feels perfect to hold you in my arms."

"For now."

"For now," he repeated softly, sadly knowing that for both of them that was all there was. Just a few days from the rest of their lives.

"And later?" she whispered, running her hand along his waist and hip.

"I don't know," he admitted.

Her lips trailed his neck and jawline. "Then let's make the very best of it," she urged between kisses, and his arms tightened, drawing her even closer to the proof of his desire.

"This *is* the best of it," he said, turning her in his arms so they could both stretch out on the couch and he could slip his hand under her bulky sweater to caress the silk of her. A soft scent wafted up that he recognized as the soap she kept in a special dish by the tub. The aroma stirred his senses, and he rubbed his palm along her pant leg.

"Ummm, do that again," she whispered.

"And this?" he asked, nuzzling the tip of her breast through her bulky sweater. "Do you like this, too?" His hand popped the snap, and with quick twist of his wrist her jeans were undone and his hand was stroking the velvety skin of her stomach.

"Turnabout is fair play," she murmured, her voice capturing him as her hands followed suit. She felt a spurt of pleasure when he groaned in delight.

They made love as if they couldn't get enough of each other: sure and quick and with more satisfaction than Honey had ever dreamed of. Now they knew the places to touch, which places to nudge, to kiss, and without conscious thought did their best to please each other.

Later, as they lay in each other's arms, the silence interrupted Honey's thoughts. Silence? She turned her head.

"What's the matter?" Beau asked sleepily.

"The rain stopped," Honey said in a monotone.

Beau stiffened, listening as if to confirm their fears. His heart plummeted. Honey was right. The rain had quit, and the wind wasn't whistling even slightly as it had the past several days. The storm was over. "No," he moaned, not really knowing what he was denying—the end of the storm or his leaving.

"Oh, Beau." Honey's sigh was a heartbreaking sound.

"Don't worry," he soothed, pulling her closely as dread crept through his bones until his entire body felt limp. But the exquisite woman in his arms made him feel warm and supple, and he turned to her to obliterate his jumbled thoughts and depression. He didn't want to think, to reason. He wanted Honey. Now.

They found their way to bed a little after midnight. Tired but contented, they held each other through the night, never losing touch with the other's warmth. Both knew they were on a path that predicted their separation, but they refused to acknowledge it.

When morning came, Honey quietly edged out of bed and made her way downstairs. She listened intently to the radio while she prepared coffee. The weather report confirmed what she already knew. The hurricane was over—and so was Beau's time with her. According to the announcer, most of the floodwater was already draining off the highways, and the sun would probably come out later.

By seven that morning she had fed the cattle, the cats and the hens, and was ready to fix breakfast. Maybe if she kept herself busy she could delay the pain she knew was coming and had no resources left to fight. No one should feel this way after just five days with a little girl and four with her father. It was wrong.

She laughed at her thoughts. Was it sex? Did she really believe that all she had been feeling was good, healthy lust? Visions of Beau flipped through her mind like the pages from a photograph album. Beau, the night he had found Meagan safe and sound. Beau, when he had picked up the shovel and begun to muck out the stall, looking every inch like a fish out of water. Beau, when he was towering over her in bed, claiming and traveling with her toward that never-never land of ecstasy.

In the beginning she had believed she was attracted to him because he was a soap star, and she had fought that furiously. Then, just as quickly, she had realized that his being a star had nothing to do with it. It was Beau himself who was the attraction. She now knew it was far more than that, but how much more she couldn't say.

No, that wasn't true. It was more like she *wouldn't* say. To speak about it aloud would give it substance, and she couldn't stand for that to linger for the rest of her life. They were incompatible. A relationship between them wouldn't work. Besides, just because she felt committed to him didn't mean that he felt the same way toward her. For all she knew she was only an intriguing interlude in his busy social life. A calm oasis in the storm.

She banged the mixing bowl down on the counter and reached for some eggs. This oasis had better get busy before she burst into tears.

The almost soundless slap of bare feet against the hardwood floor was her first warning that Beau was awake. Her eyes swung toward the kitchen door. When he seemed to fill the whole doorway, she smiled, and then found herself enveloped in his arms. Their embrace was all the more poignant because they knew he was leaving.

"I missed you when I woke up this morning," he murmured, nibbling at her ear.

"I thought I'd fix you a good old-fashioned country breakfast," she said, excusing herself for not staying in bed.

"I don't need any breakfast, Honey. I need you." His hands traveled her waist, pulling her close to him.

Her hands rose to his chest, savoring the texture of his skin. "But aren't you hungry?"

"For you," he said, lips poised above hers, his mouth barely moving as he spoke. "Only for you."

His kiss was as devastating as she had anticipated, but beneath the hand that claimed her breast she thought her heart would break. The ragged beating of her pulse seemed to confirm it. *He's leaving today. He's leaving today.* It repeated the line over and over.

"Hey," he drawled, his voice all whiskey and velvet. "What's the matter?" His hand swept away softly curling hair from the side of her face as he leaned back to look down into her eyes.

Somehow she managed to smile. "Nothing." She tried to pull away. "Scrambled eggs or an omelet?"

He tightened his hold on her. "Honey. Don't." He sounded as tortured as she felt, and she stopped, resting easily in his arms.

"Sorry," she sniffed. Her arms found their way around his back. "I'm not very good when I know there's a change in routine coming."

"Do you like the routine we make together?" he asked softly.

She nodded her lowered head, then rested it against his chest, easing her own frustration by listening to his pounding heart. "But don't worry," she said with a sigh. "We both knew this could only be a moment out of our lives. I'll be right back in my routine before you know it. And so will you."

"Will I?" he asked, kissing her temple. "I wonder."

Her arms squeezed tighter. "Three days in New York and you'll wonder how you ever stood the rigors of my boring existence as long as you did." Brave words from a woman whose heart felt as if it was breaking.

He tipped his head to the side to study her expression. "You don't really believe that, do you?"

"No," she whispered. "In fact, I hope not."

"Can I call you?"

"Yes, please."

"Can I visit?"

"No." Her tears flowed then.

He held her in his arms, rocking her as he felt the dampness on his chest and wondering why he didn't want this sad moment to end. Women dampening his chest with their tears wasn't an experience he usually cared for. But this was Honey, and Honey was crying for them both. No matter how they felt, the situation was hopeless, and they both knew it.

His arms tightened. "Could you put me up for one more day?" he asked.

Her head popped up. "You don't mean it?"

He nodded. "I've never seen Texas in sunlight, only in a downpour. Today there's sunshine."

"Wonderful."

"Wonderful."

Wonderful wasn't a big enough word to share the feelings she experienced, but it would do.

BREAKFAST WAS AN EVENT. Honey made pancakes in the shape of animals and scattered them over Meagan's plate, pretending it was a zoo. Beau laughed and joked with them without reminding Honey of the amount of sugar his daughter was consuming. It wouldn't hurt her this once. Especially not this once, as he watched Meagan glow from all the attention they lavished on her. She was like a little bloom in the warm sun of their love.

After breakfast they toured the grounds, not venturing very far because of the spongy earth. When they reached the side of the barn, Meagan's eyes widened with surprise.

"Swing!" the little girl exclaimed as she dashed under the massive oak.

"Sewing?" Honey repeated, then realized what Meagan had said. Her laughter filled the air as she recalled that first night when she had thought to teach Meagan sewing.

Meagan climbed nimbly on the low-hanging rubber tire swing, her chubby legs sticking straight out. "Push, Daddy. Push!" she insisted excitedly.

And Beau did.

They fed the animals and petted the kittens.

After dressing up, they drove into Houston, wandering the great hallways of the Galleria, window-shopping to their heart's content. Not until they stopped at a small café overlooking the indoor ice-skating rink did someone recognize Beau and ask for an autograph. Their happy closeness was dampened a bit by the intrusion, but their good spirits prevailed.

They drove down to Galveston and waded in warm Gulf waters churned gray by the storm. Meagan squealed in delight as she tried to race the waves to the shoreline. The tide was still high and there were piles of seaweed and driftwood along the beach, but the damage to the beach had been minimal.

They stopped at a small restaurant along the coast to sample raw oysters and succulent boiled shrimp, along with soft-shell crab and coleslaw. Beau and Honey sipped beers while Meagan tried to see how many Cokes she could get away with.

By sunset they were back in Honey's van, maneuvering through light traffic toward home. Honey's home.

"Meagan's asleep," Beau said softly when Honey finally pulled off the highway onto the narrow paved road leading toward Tomball.

Honey smiled. "She did a lot today."

"She had a great time."

"How about her dad? Did he enjoy it, too?"

"Her dad loved it, but kept wanting to sneak off with the chauffeur so he could ravish her beautiful body."

"The chauffeur wouldn't have minded, but Meagan might have looked funny sitting by herself in a restaurant while her daddy was busy ravishing," she said chuckling.

He gave a smile of male satisfaction. "I know. That's the only reason her father behaved himself. His choices were limited." His hand squeezed her shoulder gently, and she drove the rest of the way home careful not to dislodge it.

It was late when they pulled into the driveway. Beau carried a sleeping Meagan into the house. They deposited her into bed, sand and all.

They stood for a moment at the door, the dim lamp from the hall the only light penetrating the dark room. Beau's arms wrapped around Honey's waist as they leaned against each other, silent because words couldn't convey what he was feeling. Only touching her could do that.

"Honey," he murmured and she twisted around in his arms.

She pressed her fingers against his lips, her brown eyes liquid with love and desire. "Shhh," she said in a whisper he could barely make out. "Don't say anything. Show me."

He kissed her finger, taking the tip into his mouth, sucking gently as he watched a myriad of emotions cross her face. His body stiffened with the urge to provide the strength they both would need in the morning. But now . . . now he needed her more than he needed to breathe.

Honey, who had the wits and the will to survive alone far from help or neighbors. Honey, who knew so much about being alone and so little about men and women. Honey, who managed so well when away from people but who would wither if surrounded by them.

His arms clutched her possessively as he gave her back her finger in favor of her slightly parted lips. He knew there was no way for them to stay together, but he wasn't ready for the parting, either.

Honey. His Honey. His sweet, golden Honey for tonight. Nothing else mattered except this night, this moment, this woman.

8

HONEY PERCHED ON THE FENCE watching the cattle graze contentedly on the fresh grass. An occasional lowing drifted through the spring air. The warm Texas sun was shining down as it had for the past week. A gentle breeze fluttered across the pasture, lifting a few strands of her hair and playing with it before letting it rest again on her shoulders.

Her jeans were clean, her shirt was crisp, her weathered Stetson sat jauntily on her head. Only her grave expression suggested that her mood didn't match the quiet pastoral scene. Loneliness enfolded her in a musty, wet blanket, chilling her when she should have been basking in the warmth of the day.

Beau and Meagan had left for Austin on the second sunny day, just as she had known they would. Their leave-taking was quiet, a prediction of her future, except that they had left behind ghosts that taunted her with their laughter.

Beau had kissed her gently while she had slept, had bundled up a sleepy Meagan and had left, with only a brief note to tell her of his thoughts.

She had cried over that note. So much that only a crumpled piece of ink-stained paper remained as evidence. But it didn't matter; she had memorized the message:

This was the best way. Hold that kiss until I see you again. I miss you already.

Love, Beau and Meagan.

She clung to the thought of seeing him again, even though she knew better. Beau belonged to another life, one that didn't include her. It never could. She knew as well as he that neither of them could survive in the other's world. They were worlds apart.

Theirs had been a match made in hell, a cruel joke the gods had played just to see what would happen. And what had? For one thing, she had died a little inside. No, a lot. She had also grown wiser.

If Peter hadn't fallen in love again and had stayed with her on the farm, that relationship still wouldn't have worked out. They would have ended up in divorce court—and not entirely because of Peter. That was hard for her to accept, but it was the truth.

She had been unwilling and unable to bend then, to meet him even halfway. His main fault was that he had known from the beginning rural life wasn't for him. He had assumed she would cheerfully live in the city with him, just as she was convinced he would eventually share country living with her. But neither one had even voiced that view to the other. Looking back, she realized they'd had their own dreams and perhaps had even sensed secretly the other couldn't share them. That had stifled any communication even more. When Peter's ex-girlfriend had shown up, he and Honey had already grown so far apart that it was only logical for him to seek love elsewhere.

Strangely, she had never been able to see that until now. She sighed deeply. Was it her personality, some deficiency in her that made her choose to love men who were so wrong for her? For she knew now that she loved Beau with all her heart. And the feeling was far beyond her ability to stop or alter it.

She shifted on the rail. He wasn't coming back. Even if he did, it would be just another visit and he'd be off again, back to his world, where he could breathe and live and grow. Beau had chosen his lifestyle as she had chosen hers.

But she couldn't stop watching him every day on TV. And every day a mixture of depression and joy did battle in her soul. Watching was the closest she could get to him.

Without noticing the flock of birds flying back north for the summer, she hopped lithely to the ground and headed for the house. It was time to get back to work.

She adjusted the books for a local hardware store until almost one o'clock that morning, stopping only to drink more coffee. All her professional ability was called upon to sort through the owner's crude book-keeping to make it conform to an acceptably orderly pattern.

By two a.m. she was wandering the hallways, too pumped up with caffeine and too confused by her mixed-up thoughts to consider sleep.

When the phone rang, she grabbed for it, knowing instinctively that it was Beau.

"Hello, Honey." His voice was velvet, stroking her ear and transmitting sensual, intimate messages through her body. "How are you?"

Honey could hear the muted echos of other voices drifting through the receiver. Was he at a party, or were the lines crossed somewhere? "Where are you?" she asked breathlessly.

"I'm at home, taking refuge in Meagan's bedroom. My sister, Shelly, is having a party." He sounded weary, almost exhausted.

"You're calling me in the middle of a party?"

"I needed to hear your voice." No excuses. His statement's meaning washed over her in warm waves.

She tried to pull her scattered emotions together. "How's Meagan?" she managed finally, kicking herself for not being able to tell him all the things she had been thinking.

"She's sound asleep in the other bed, but she misses you almost as much as I do," he said, his voice filled with longing.

"How much?" she found herself asking, praying he would supply the words that would help her endure the next week's emptiness.

"Too damn much. You intrude on my every thought." Was that an admission of her presence in his life? She didn't know.

Her hand gripped the receiver even tighter against her ear. "Tell me," she pleaded in a throaty whisper.

"Every time I turn around, I'm looking for you. In the street, at work, at a party. But you aren't there."

"I'm here," she said.

"I know. And that's too far away," he said huskily. "Just when I think I've stopped looking for you, Meagan will say your name with just the same longing I'm feeling, and it brings you back to me in full force."

"We don't match, Beau," she finally got out.

"I know," he admitted raggedly. "We're all wrong."

"All wrong," she repeated sorrowfully.

"I can't help it, Honey. I want you anyway. I need you. Dark nights and early mornings aren't the same without you. They'll never be the same." His voice revealed the fatigue of fighting that very admission . . . before inevitably admitting it.

"But we don't fit," she whispered achingly.

His sigh echoed over the long-distance line. "My head knows that, but my heart doesn't. I can't convince it not to crave you at odd hours of the day."

"That's sex."

"No, that's love," he corrected her firmly. "Right or wrong."

She hesitated only for a moment. "I know," she finally admitted.

"Come to New York, Honey. Stay with me," he demanded, his voice once more sure and strong.

"No," was her soft answer and he understood more from that one word than he had from their whole conversation.

"We can *make* it work."

"No."

"Yes!" he exploded, frustration honing the sharp edges of his anger. "Neither of us can go on like this. We shouldn't have to. Dammit! It's only land, Honey! Not flesh and blood and emotions that keep you warm at night!"

Her cry was a plea for help. "And I would die in your world, just as you would in mine! Can't you see that? We've both made the same stupid mistake again! Let's not compound it." She didn't want to consider what might happen if Pamela were to show up again, but that small, niggling possibility was always there, eating at her constantly.

So the silence was her answer. They both knew she was right.

"I love you, Honey."

"I love you, too." Her words were wrenched from deep inside.

And then the line went dead.

Honey was too emotionally drained to even cry. She curled up in the corner of the couch in the darkened living room, remembering his every move and every word he had spoken to her.

BEAU LEANED BACK on the pillow, hands behind his head, staring at the ceiling of the dimly lit bedroom. The small lamp beside the bed sent up a shaft of softened light to illuminate the textured finish of the plaster.

Honey. His thoughts had been consumed with her ever since he had returned a week ago. Food didn't taste the same, the beautiful women he knew didn't look as fresh or as inside-beautiful as Honey. They wore their makeup like war paint and discussed thoroughly mundane topics as if their lives depended on them. They flitted about like bees to flowers, afraid they would miss the pollen of good, juicy gossip.

Honey. In a sense she reminded him of all the wonderful things he had once missed and still craved in his life. Once, long ago, he had prayed for parents who were kept on schedule by routine, right down to cookies and milk after school or before bedtime. A sense of order he and Shelly had never had and secretly had always dreamed of.

No surrogate parent who was a bachelor uncle could provide that kind of family life, no matter how hard he tried. By necessity, their routine was an organizational one, similar to a large, impersonal corporation—supposedly for the good of everyone concerned. His uncle had never had children of his own or been around them, and although he never mistreated Beau and Shelly, the little elements of love, affection, caring and compassion were missing. That same lack ensured that Beau and Shelly remained close to each other.

When he had first encountered Honey's "routine," he'd thought he would go insane from the mere idea of it. But in the space of a day he'd realized how nice it was to know he would eat at certain times, that even the cats and chickens were to be fed according to schedule. Even her cleaning had an order to it. He liked that. While the rest of the world went crazy, he had been in a safe, structured place with Honey and Meagan.

But it was much more than that.

In another surprising sense she was his cornerstone—the epitome of everything purely feminine he'd known but without the fripperies of sexy underwear, sensual perfume from a fancy bottle and flirting because it was expected. Honey wasn't any of those things, yet in the days they had shared he had found her to be one of the most sensuous, feminine women he had ever known. Even her own natural body scent turned him on.

He loved her.

He knew it, and yet there wasn't a damn thing he could do about it. Frustration roiled his insides, and he settled for movement as a way to escape, pulling himself off the bed just as Shelly opened the door, then closed it quickly behind her as she leaned her back against it.

She stared at her brother with concern. "All right, big brother. What's going on?" She spoke in a stage whisper so Meagan wouldn't stir. Her hands rested on her hips as she dared him to utter the answer he had been giving her all week—a grouchy grunt.

"Nothing." He tucked his shirt back into his waistband.

"Come on, give! Claudia has been out there batting her eyelashes off trying to get your attention, and you're in here sulking. Usually you'd be flirting back by now. Instead you're on the phone, and I have a feeling that you were talking to 'Texas.'" That was Shelly's name for Honey. "What's going on?"

He grunted his usual reply to that statement, one brow raised in question. Shelly moved farther into the room. "You do know that if Meagan were acting this way you'd have a fit."

"I'm not Meagan." He ran a hand around the back of his neck, rubbing away the tension. What he really wanted was a good swig of Honey's whiskey. "I'm just tired." What he really wanted was Honey. With him.

Shelly nodded, her eyes luminous with worry that had consumed her in the past week. "I know. You've been listless since you got back." She wandered over to the bed and sat down, crossing her legs as she stared at her hands folded in her lap. "Don't you even want to talk about it?"

"No." His voice was curt, his manner more abrupt than he had ever used with her before. Until he looked at her. "I'm sorry, Shel," he said with a sigh. "I just need some time by myself." He sat down on the bed next to her, his hand reaching out to hold hers. "This party wasn't quite the right answer for me," he added ruefully, thinking of the women out there who were so plastic compared to Honey.

"You used to enjoy them. That's why I invited everybody. To cheer you up." Shelly's voice was low with hurt.

"You invited them because you were in the mood for a party, Shelly. It didn't have a whole lot to do with me, did it?" He stood up resignedly. "So let's go out and pretend we're enjoying it for the sake of our guests."

Beau opened the door and walked into the arms of Claudia just as a new song began on the stereo. Claudia never noticed his weary sigh as his arms came around her and they danced around the room.

His eyes skimmed the crowd. He wished more than anything he were on a plane for Houston. Instead, he'd be in Los Angeles within the week to audition for a role in a new TV spy series. If it went well, he'd be able to leave this behind and begin anew on the West Coast.

Begin what? his mind chided. He'd still be too far away from Honey.

ALMOST EVERY NIGHT after that, Honey got a phone call from Beau. At first, she was reluctant to talk, afraid to reveal her thoughts or to describe the humdrum life she led. Then, slowly, she realized he enjoyed listening to her as much as she loved living his glittery life vicariously.

"Do you remember Samsonia, the hen?" Honey asked, curled up in bed with the phone perched on her shoulder. "Well, she hatched an egg, and a darling little chick came out, a carbon copy of her mother, only covered with down instead of feathers."

"I bet guineas are cuter as babies than grown-ups," he said with a chuckle.

"You're right. But Momma didn't take care and walked through a puddle. Baby followed right along behind and almost drowned."

"What happened?"

"I rescued her, but now I'm worried about pneumonia. She's in a box at the foot of my bed, up to her neck in shredded paper and cuddled against a warm rock."

"I wish I was at the foot of your bed," Beau said, his voice dropping an octave.

"With a warm rock?" she teased.

When he told her what he thought of that idea, she blushed, unable to curb the giggle that got away from her.

"Do you remember me telling you about my director, Len?" Beau asked.

"Oh, yes, the man who discovered you." Honey said, tongue in cheek. "How could someone discover you? Weren't you always there?" she asked laughing.

Beau chuckled. "Never mind, smartie. Anyway, he got me into that new disco that opened on Seventh Avenue, and the following morning my picture was plastered all over the papers. So, if you see it, don't believe it."

"What's it say?" she asked, pretending that she couldn't guess. But her heart sank anyway.

"It says I'm in love with my leading lady. Only it's nonsense because she's happily married and has two children."

"Oh." She was more relieved than she cared to let on.

They talked about the filming of his soap, and he explained how he was being written out. "Then I'll be in Los Angeles for the next two weeks. If everything goes well, we'll be moving out there."

Her voice was warm with pride. "That's wonderful. Now I can say I know a really successful star."

"Don't soap opera stars count?" he teased.

Her laughter disappeared. "On the contrary. Sometimes they count too much."

"Oh, Honey." He said her name in a way that told her so much.

"I know," she whispered, her voice broken by the same thoughts as his.

This was a dangerous game they were playing, and she knew it. It would only lead to heartache. For them, there was no possible future, but neither seemed able to let go.

He told her the private investigator had finally tracked Pamela down. She was in Brownsville, Texas, still living with the man she had left New York with. That was the end of the investigation. Beau had declined to lay any charges.

In the back of Honey's mind was always the troubling thought that, if Pamela changed and came back into his life, Beau would accept her. Surely they had been through too much together for him not to care, at least a little.

For two weeks, Honey listened for Beau's calls. Sometimes he would call at six in the evening, sometimes not before one or two in the morning, but he called every night.

She had to smile at some of their conversations, because if anyone ever listened to them, they would certainly have thought them bizarre. Politics, child care, cooking, even religion came up, sometimes in agreement, occasionally in heated argument. Most people met and got to know each other on dates, over lunch, during face-to-face encounters. Beau and

Honey learned about each other over long-distance wires.

But not until Beau's phone call a few days later did she realize how very much she loved him. Three days earlier he had left for California. His audition had gone off without a hitch, but he was still worried. The state of mind of producers and directors was always an unknown factor and often as much a mystery to mortal man as moviegoers' tastes were to the executives.

"Honey! I got the part!" Beau shouted into the phone. "It's a spy series with a great leading character, and it looks like we've got the best writers in the business!"

She laughed at his exuberance. "Wonderful! Now what?"

"Now Meagan and Shelly move out here and I begin shooting in two weeks."

"Where will you live?" Honey asked. She had only moved twice in her life, and both times had been an ordeal.

Beau chuckled, understanding her fear of a less than ordered life. "Somewhere. Anywhere. A town house. A rental house. An apartment. We'll make do until I can take time off to find what I really want."

"But Meagan . . ." Honey began, only to fall silent.

"Darling, don't worry," he reassured her softly. "I'm not worried about Meagan. She'll still have our housekeeper, Shelly and me. I'm more interested in you." His declaration was met with no response, because Honey didn't know what to say. She heard him take a deep breath. "Honey, come out here. Stay with me for a little while. See what you think of California."

"I can't." Her throat closed tight. But he had asked! He had actually asked. She had no choice but to refuse.

"Yes, you can. Two weeks is all I ask."

"I can't." Didn't he understand they had only been playing a game these past weeks and that they were merely prolonging the inevitable?

"Yes, you can," he said, with more conviction than he felt.

"No."

"Yes. One week."

"Yes," she sighed.

"Good," he said matter-of-factly, barely managing to hide his triumph. "I'll make the arrangements. Be ready to leave in two days."

"That's too soon," she groaned, mentally reviewing everything she had to do before leaving.

"Two days," he said firmly, his fingers itching to hold her. "That's time enough. Any more and you'll figure out a thousand reasons why you can't come."

"All right, but only if I can bring Sandals for Meagan," she said bargaining with a smile.

Beau chuckled. "You know you've got me between a rock and a hard place, don't you?"

This time she giggled. "Yes."

He sighed, but she knew he wasn't really annoyed. "Okay," he said softly. "I'll see you soon, my love." He hung up before she could change her mind.

HER FIRST FLIGHT was exciting but not half as thrilling as the thought of being with Beau and Meagan again. It was still hard for her to believe that she'd agreed to come, let alone to travel by herself to meet a man she had no future with. She was crazy... but for once she felt heady and excited. She felt *alive*!

The Los Angeles airport was jammed with bodies, but no crowd could screen Beau's tall, lean body from her sight. He stood in the arrival lounge, as handsome and virile as she remembered him. In white slacks and a white-and-green polo shirt, he looked as if he had lived on the West Coast all his life instead of just two weeks. In seconds her gift for Meagan was sitting on the floor and she was in his arms being swirled around the lobby.

Light, tinkling laughter erupted from her as he lowered her feet to the ground, but his hands were tight on her waist. Brown and green eyes filled with unspoken promises, meeting and holding, sharing and speaking their desires more plainly than words.

He bent toward her, his lips finding the curve of her ear. "You made it, lady, and tonight we'll celebrate by not leaving our bed!" he whispered only for her ears to hear.

Her hands cradled his jaw as she pretended to glare at him, knowing he could feel her heartbeat quicken at his intimate invitation. "I flew all this way never to see more than the four walls of a bedroom?"

His green eyes lit with mischief. "You'll never be bored enough to notice the four walls. I have more important things to show you, my lady."

"Promises, promises," she bubbled, feeling younger than she ever had. Beau was her Disneyland, her wonder ride. He made her live as she had never dared to before.

When his lips touched hers, she closed her eyes with sheer ecstasy. Her arms reached for his shoulders, then twined around his neck, loving the demands of his kiss and wanting it never to end. When he lifted his head, she stared up at him, her golden-brown eyes slightly unfocused. He smoothed her tawny hair, tucking a vagrant strand behind her ear. His smile was indulgent. "It looks like you brought enough trouble with you in that little case." He nodded toward the kitten curled up asleep in the carrier.

"She's no trouble at all. Look how cute she is," Honey teased, lifting the case to eye level.

"She's cute and she's female. That spells trouble," Beau declared, taking her arm and leading her toward the baggage-claim area. "But if she comes along with you, then I'll shut up. I'll take you any way I can. A cat, ten cats, ten head of cattle. It doesn't matter."

Honey's heart felt lighter than air. Nothing between them had changed.

After Honey's luggage was found and the car was brought around, a new black Mercedes, they were on their way.

They drove for almost an hour before turning into a steep drive somewhere in Beverly Hills. The streets wound around, showing off all the houses in the area. From the outside, each looked much like the other, and Honey's eyes darted about as she wondered which was his, until Beau pulled into a narrow driveway and buzzed the garage door opener.

"Home," he announced as he opened his door and walked around to Honey's side. As soon as she slipped out of the seat, he pulled her into his arms. "Welcome to California, and to me, my Honey," he said before claiming a kiss that made her legs weak with wanting.

Someone cleared her throat, and they broke apart, Beau frowning and Honey clearly embarrassed.

Shelly's laughter filled the air. "Stop frowning, Beau, or you'll look old before your time. You can talk to Texas later, but now it's time for me to get to meet her." Shelly stretched out her hand, clasping Honey's warmly. "So you're the lady who's larger than life."

Honey glanced at Beau, confused. "I beg your pardon?"

"Beau and Meagan haven't been able to talk about anything unless your name was sprinkled throughout the conversation," Shelly teased, delighting in her brother's discomfort.

"Okay, Shelly," he said gruffly. "Say your hellos and forget the exposé," he warned, but Honey could sense immediately the camaraderie they shared.

"Yes, sir." Shelly grinned, giving him a mock salute. "It's just that it's so much fun to ride you for a change. Usually, it's the other way around."

They walked into the house, Honey enjoying the banter between them, obviously the result of a lifetime's practice. Their genuine caring and warmth was evident.

"I took Meagan to school today, even though she wanted to stay home and wait for you," Shelly explained as she and Honey went into the living room while Beau brought the luggage from the car. "She would have been frantic waiting all morning for you."

"How is she?"

Shelly chuckled. "As precocious as ever. And missing you. Beau and Meagan have been fighting for president of your fan club."

"I'm pretty fond of them, too."

"You'd better be," Beau announced from the doorway, her suitcases in his hands, green eyes glinting with clear meaning, and Honey blushed. He put the suitcases at the bottom of the steps and entered the room.

Shelly laughed. She stood up and walked toward the doorway. "I'll see you later, Honey. Right now, I'd better see what we're going to have for dinner. Meagan will be home in a couple of hours, and she's always starving lately. I think it's a habit she picked up in Houston."

After Shelly left, the room was silent. She stared at Beau, studying him intently for several long seconds, assuring herself that she was really here. With him.

Beau searched her face, finding the faint remnant of her blush delightful. Silently he took her in his arms. Then his lips came down to capture hers, showing her his idea of a real welcome kiss.

An hour later Honey was ensconced in the guest room, her bags unpacked and her limbs invaded by a happy tiredness borne of the excitement of the trip. At the foot of her bed was the little carrier with webbing on its sides. Sandals was curled up on a thick, square piece of felt, still quiet from the light tranquilizer Honey had given her earlier.

She heard horns honk and neighbors' dogs yelping, and somewhere nearby there was a pool party in full swing.

From the window she stared at the palm garden below. Its obvious beauty was foreign to her eye in plan and terrain compared to her small farm. Homes crowded upon homes all over the hillside, marching in rows into the valley. Everything looked so different. A tiny stab of homesickness pricked her for a moment, but she shook it off. When it was time to leave, she would hate to part from Beau just as much as she had hated to leave her land, even for a short while.

She knew when he came into her room; her radar still worked perfectly. He came up behind her and wrapped his arms around her waist, his hands coming together just below the fullness of her breasts. She leaned her head against the solid comfort of his chest as they both looked out the window. Suddenly the tinge of homesickness was replaced by a feeling of peace. She closed her eyes to keep it close, never so much at home as she was at that minute.

"I've dreamed of you being here, with me." His voice was warm syrup over her senses, and she leaned into him even more.

"I've dreamed of being here, too."

"With me or just in California?" he asked knowing the answer but wanting to hear it from her.

"With you," she admitted with a satisfied sigh.

"And what did you dream of doing?"

"Having you hold me, just like you are now."

"What?" His lips brushed her earlobe. "No kisses, no caresses? Just holding?"

"Mmmm," she said, tipping her head around to give him better access. "For starters, anyway."

"Then what?" He kissed the nape of her neck, his lips barely brushing the softness there.

"Then we'd make love, slow and easy."

"Just once?" His lips traveled up her cheek to her temple, his tongue finding her quickening pulse.

"No." Her voice was a croak.

"How many times?"

"Several."

He turned her around in his arms and looked down at her, love and tenderness pouring from his deep green eyes. "Then I suggest we begin right away."

"Why?" she asked, loving the way his mouth moved.

His arms tightened as he pulled her against his evident arousal. The teasing tone was gone. "Because I don't think I can wait. I need you so much, Honey."

He didn't wait for her reply. His lips claimed hers in a kiss that told her everything. He hugged her even closer to him, as if afraid she might disappear.

And they renewed the love that had grown despite the distance between them.

His loving was slow and gentle, just as Honey had prophesied. Beau held back until beads of perspiration dotted his forehead, but it was worth it. As she melted in his arms, the touch of her was silk and satin across his skin. Every nerve in his body hummed in harmony with the tune she played. But he found sustenance and revenge at her breast, paying her back for the sweet torture she had put him through and receiving more in kind.

"Do you like this?" he asked, his fingertips tracing her body.

"Yes."

"And this?" His hands slipped down to explore all the secret places he remembered so well.

"Yes."

"And this?"

"Stop talking," she whispered. "I'll let you know what year to stop."

"Yes, ma'am," he said before slipping off her opened blouse and skirt, then quickly dispensing with his own clothes. "I aim to please, ma'am."

"Then aim well, Mr. McGuire," she ordered in a whisper.

When they came together, it was if they had been born to fit that way. And after soaring to the heights of their passion, they found simple peace and quiet contentment entwined in each other's arms.

9

IT WASN'T UNTIL EARLY EVENING that she saw Meagan. Honey had showered and put on a new, casual outfit of tan pants with white piping and a matching tan-and-white nubby cotton sweater. She was applying mascara, thinking of Beau's intimate, parting smile as he had reluctantly left her room, when there was a knock on the door.

"Momma?" Too impatient to wait for an answer, the little girl opened the door and peeked around the corner. Her small heart-shaped face was lit with pleasure. Without another word, she ran across the room and dived into Honey's open arms.

"I knew you would come an' see me," she declared into Honey's lap.

Honey gave her a light squeeze. "And did you think I'd come alone?" Honey asked softly.

Meagan's face lifted. Her bright green eyes were puzzled. "Who did you bring?" she asked.

"Well," Honey began, "there was this little kitten who kept crying for her friend. I didn't know how to make her happy, except to bring her with me."

Meagan's eyes were saucers. "Really?"

Honey nodded. "Look behind you in that case on the floor."

In an instant, Meagan was out of Honey's arms and down on all fours in front of the carrier. Honey had to smile. It was all too easy to be replaced by a kitten in a child's affection....

Before long Meagan was sitting cross-legged in the center of Honey's bed gently patting the groggy kitten that was curled in her lap like a fluffy, furry ball.

"Will Daddy be mad?" Meagan asked hesitantly.

"No, darlin'," she said smiling. "I told him before I brought Sandals to live with you. He agreed that you needed each other."

Her big green eyes were relieved. "Now I have you *and* Sandals!" Her smile was as bright as the sun.

"I'm just visiting," Honey explained carefully as she sat on the side of the bed and scratched the kitten's chin. "But when I leave, you'll still have Sandals. You'll have to learn to feed her every day and care for her by keeping the litter box clean and making sure she always has water. That's a big job. Do you think you can handle it?"

Meagan nodded, eager to begin her new duty. "I can take care of my own room, 'cept for making my bed," she declared, as if impressing on Honey the extent of her already awesome responsibilities. "So I can take care of Sandals."

"Good, darlin'," Honey said. "Now let's go downstairs and see if we can help with dinner." She held out her hand. Meagan carefully placed the sleepy kitten in the center of the bed, then took Honey's hand, and they left the room together.

If only everything could be solved as easily as Sandals's life . . .

Dinner was fun. Being a member of a close-knit family was unusual for Honey, but she liked it.

Meagan regaled them with stories about her new preschool and the friends she had made.

"An' Bobby punched him in the nose for me!" Meagan said with the satisfaction of one who had seen justice done.

"But it wasn't nice for Bobby to punch him, Meagan. Bobby wasn't the one who got hit in the first place," Shelly said, trying to explain the rudiments of fighting etiquette.

"But *I* couldn't punch him!" Meagan declared with unerring logic. "He's too big!"

Honey couldn't help the laughter that spilled out as she listened to Meagan's tales of a day at nursery school. Obviously things hadn't changed much since she'd been a girl.

But Shelly's conversation surprised her the most. It seemed Beau's sister had the impression he and Honey were going to be together for some time.

Hadn't Beau explained to Shelly that this was just an interlude for them? She tried to bring it up several times, but the lump in her throat refused to let her speak. Besides, basking in the warm glow from Beau's eyes, she couldn't think clearly about anything.

This was just a brief vacation, she kept reminding herself. But her efforts didn't seem to be working....

Meagan was glued to her side as they went into the living room, hugging Honey's hand in both of hers as they sat on the couch. Shelly had cleared the table and was in the kitchen, loading the dishwasher.

"She missed you a lot," Beau said quietly, sitting on the other side of her and bending forward to whisper in her ear.

"I missed her, too," Honey said.

Meagan simply sat there, her head resting against Honey's arm, her eyes dancing between the two adults. She smiled winningly, looking like a miniature of her father whenever he turned on the charm. "Can I play with Sandals in the kitchen?" she asked, pleading. "I'll be good."

"Go, moppet. Just don't make a mess," Beau warned, and Honey wondered what could happen from playing with a kitten in a kitchen. She decided not to ask.

His hand enfolded the nape of her neck, pulling her gently toward him. "I still can't believe you're here with me," he murmured. "I have to keep touching you to make sure you're not a figment of my imagination."

She leaned her head against the curve of his shoulder. "I can't believe it, either," she admitted, her heart beating rapidly. "But it feels so good."

His eyes darkened. "Shelly's moving out next month. She's found an apartment."

Honey stared at him, waiting for what he was going to say and hoping that he wouldn't.

But he did. "Stay with me, Honey. Come live here. Let's be a family. Together."

Her eyes glistened with unshed tears. Damn him! Did he always have to have things his way? "That's not fair," she whispered brokenly. "Not to any of us, but especially not to me."

"I can't get you any other way."

"Would you move to the country with me? Would you give up everything you have to spend your days on the farm?" Her voice was choked, but her message was clear. He was asking her to give up everything her life stood for, while he'd continue on as he was.

A groan passed his lips, and he reached out to hold her tightly, his face buried in her hair. "I'm sorry, Honey," he said with a tremor. "I love you and I want you with me. That's all."

She shook her head, unable to speak. She couldn't give up everything she knew just to be here for Beau and Meagan. She had already tried once and had learned the hard way that nothing was forever.

"Think about it. Let's see what happens this week," he finally muttered, pulling back to gently wipe a tear from her cheek. "Who knows? A miracle might happen."

A miracle. That's what it would take. As much as she loved him, she knew she'd be returning to Houston at the end of the week. He knew that, too. His eyes proved it.

FOR THE FIRST TWO DAYS they made a world of their own and closed the doors on the rest of civilization. It was as if they were back at Honey's farm all over again. Shelly came and went, busily applying for jobs at different schools. The housekeeper, Mrs. Adams, was quiet as a mouse. Honey, Meagan and Beau shared an enchanted cottage.

It was on the third day at lunchtime that Honey was bumped out of the enchantment and pushed into reality.

"There's a party tonight that I have to go to. Can you be ready by eight?" Beau's voice was casual, his eyes never rising above the barley-and-herb soup.

Honey's spoon paused in midair. "Me?"

"Yes, you." He lifted the spoon to his lips, pretending he was savoring the taste. "I have to go, but I don't want to go without you."

"I'm afraid you'll have to. I didn't bring anything dressy with me."

"Then we'll go find something for you this afternoon."

"I don't want to." Honey placed her spoon carefully on her plate, waiting for him to look up so she could impress upon him her firm decision. Her pulse quickened in sheer terror. All those people, none of whom she knew. And they all knew Beau.

He continued to study his soup.

"Beau?"

"What?" At last he glanced up. "I was just thinking."

"Then, while you're at it, please think again about not taking me to that party."

"Honey." Beau paused. His expression closed completely, and his eyes grew distant. "I want you there. I stayed at your farm for five days, doing what you did. Now I want you to see my side of life."

Honey managed another sip of her soup. She knew either they were going to have an argument or she was going to give in. "If you insist," she said, unwilling to admit how terrified she had become of parties, going only when she had to. Here it would be worse—she would be totally out of her element.

He stared at her as if trying to read her mind. "When I asked you out here, I knew there'd be parties I'd have to attend, publicity I'd have to do."

Her brows rose. "And you asked me anyway?"

"Yes." He nodded, his eyes piercing hers. "I wanted you with me no matter what."

Her hands coiled into angry fists in her lap. "Why didn't you tell me?"

"Would you have come if I had?" he asked quietly.

"No . . ." she began.

"That's why." He slid back his chair and stood, his broad physique so imposing she could hardly breathe. "I want you to see the way I live just as you made me see your way." He moved around the table and took her hands in his, lifting her toward him, his eyes searching hers for understanding. "I was selfish. I wanted you with me regardless."

When his lips claimed hers, any thought of argument fled. Still, deep down, she knew it wouldn't work. Not just because she still doubted that he had come to terms with Pamela. What would happen if she were ever to step back into his life?

When they arrived at the party that evening, her unspoken fears had rendered her quiet and withdrawn. Beau's hand reached for hers across the car seat. "I promise you it won't be as bad as it was for Joan of Arc when the fire was lit."

Honey couldn't control her smile. "Promise?" Suddenly the chic copper-shot dress they had purchased that afternoon didn't seem to be the perfect fit, the perfect foil, the perfect dress she had thought it was. Her self-confidence was disappearing fast.

But Beau didn't notice. He nodded. "You bet. And I won't leave your side, or let anyone carrying torches anywhere near you. We'll be Siamese twins."

Her sense of humor was returning. "In front of everyone?"

He chuckled and planted a soft kiss on her lips. "Even the president, if he's there."

The party was on the second floor of a large building at the studio. Muffled merriment and faint music could be heard when they opened the car doors. Chin up and back straight, Honey walked close to Beau's side as they entered the building and waited for the elevator. His analogy of Joan of Arc hadn't been too far off the mark. She felt cold all over except where Beau's hand rested on the gentle slope of her back.

"Relax," he whispered. "I'll get this damn publicity out of the way and then we'll leave," he promised, wishing he could kiss away her fears. She didn't realize that he had a few fears of his own that needed soothing.

By the time the elevator arrived at the party floor, the noise was loud enough to wake the dead. The room was decorated with several sets that she recognized from TV shows. Large spotlights were strung from catwalks near the ceilings. The effect wasn't exactly cozy; in fact, it was positively intimidating, reminding her of the glamour that surrounded making movies and television series. It was her first startled glimpse of a world with which she was totally unfamiliar.

An eight-piece band blared from one corner, but to insure that everyone had an equal opportunity to be deafened, large speakers were scattered in the other corners of the huge room.

Women in sleek dresses that revealed more than they covered stood with drinks in their hands and canned laughter pouring from their carmined mouths. Men in stylish tuxedos were next to their women, tossing back as many cold drinks as they could, hoping against hope that the air-conditioning would begin to cool off the large room filled to the rafters with humanity.

The perfect Hollywood party on the perfect Hollywood set.

"Beau! Beau McGuire!" an older man bellowed, uncurling the fingers of the woman next to him from his arm as he tried to reach them. "It's about time you got here. Hastings has been waiting for you. He's got a gossip columnist with him, and he wants to make sure you're mentioned." Even while the man was talking, his eyes were assessing Honey, a warm glow revealing to Beau that he approved wholeheartedly.

Beau gritted his teeth and made the introduction. "Honey, this is Hank Fairchild, producer of the show I'll be doing. Hank, Honey Carter."

"How do you do," she murmured as she accepted his hand.

"A Southern accent. That's good. Very good," Fairchild said, more to himself than to them. "Wait until Hastings gets a load of it. He'll love it."

Beau schooled his expression, allowing only a small smile to show as he cocked one eyebrow in silent question.

"You know, Beau," Hank explained. "For publicity. Nothing like a Southern accent to go with our Boy of the Hour."

Beau led her away from Hank toward the makeshift bar in the corner opposite from the band.

Several times along the way, people stopped Beau to shake his hand or give him a pat on the back, but he wasn't as eager to introduce them to Honey as they were to meet her. She realized he was trying to protect her at the same time he was using her as a shield, and she couldn't help relaxing when she saw he was even more nervous than she was. She could understand it. Her career wasn't on the line, only her dislike of large crowds.

He ordered a Scotch on the rocks for himself and turned to ask silently what she wanted.

With a slight smile, she checked what the other women were drinking. "White wine, please," she said primly.

"Going on the wagon?" His eyes twinkled.

"If I'm going to be entertaining as well as be entertained, I'd better keep a clear head."

"Ready for the dragons?" He nodded toward a large table to one side. The five men seated there looked as if they were royalty being fawned upon by their loyal subjects.

"Ready when you are." She smiled, swallowing her nervousness.

Honey took a deep breath as they approached the table where his director and the latest, top-of-the-heap gossip columnist sat. "Honey, I'd like you to meet the man who insists he discovered me, German Hastings." Beau's green eyes glinted with mirth as he stood over the portly older man whose eyes fairly popped in frank admiration of Honey. "German, meet Honey Carter."

Discovered Beau? Well, she had discovered him, too. . . .

It was way past midnight before they were on their way home. Honey relaxed against the soft leather cushions of the Mercedes and let a hearty sigh escape.

"Tired?" Beau's voice was dark gray velvet that washed over her body.

"Exhausted."

"You were the hit of the party, you know."

"No," she corrected. "You were the hit. I was the hit's mystery guest."

"We made quite a team." His voice was light with satisfaction. He was more than content with Honey at his side. He refused to think what it would be like to have to attend the next hundred parties and not have her with him. Only one word came to mind— *boring*.

His arm circled her shoulders possessively, pulling her closer as he drove the last part of the way home. His body repsonded instantly to her nearness, and his insides ached with the desire to have her beside him always. The silence in the car was as sweet and loving as their words usually were.

She reached up to caress the side of his jaw. "What are you thinking?"

"About us."

"Oh?"

He gave a dark chuckle laced with frustration. "I'm wondering how often I can spend the summers with you and how often you can spend the winters with me. I envision us trying to meet each other in airports when we're old and gray. We'll still be doggedly spending half our time traveling just to be together."

Her hand stilled. "Or maybe you'll find a bathing beauty queen who will love you and take good care of you. Then those trips will dwindle—"

"Stop it." His voice was harsh. "There is no one else. There never will be. Just you."

She couldn't help saying out loud what she had been thinking for weeks, regardless of how little he wanted to hear it. "But it's true, Beau. Sooner or later you'll find someone who does fit your way of life. It might even be someone you already know. And when you do, this will all be just an interlude. A memory."

"No. You are my chosen way of life," he said firmly, anger at her commonsense attitude sharpening his words. His arm tightened, bringing her closer, and she didn't try to pull back. The inside of the car sang with the quiet. At last, when Beau spoke, his voice was tight with emotion. "I love you, Honey. No one can take your place. And I'll be damned if I can see how I can do without us being us."

Her hand smoothed the furrows from his forehead, longing to ease the pain he showed so plainly and she felt so deeply. "Shhh," she whispered. "We'll see, darling." But in her heart she knew she felt as he did.

She remembered that one time during the storm she had wished to be glamorous for Beau. Well, if the looks she had received tonight were anything to go by, she had her wish. Everyone she'd met had been more than gracious. Her dress had been perfect. And she'd also found she could survive in his climate. She didn't like it, but she could endure it—at least for a night or two. But she was sure a steady diet would wear her down until there was nothing left.

Later that night, in the quiet of her darkened room, Beau came to her and made love as if she were the essence of life itself.

"Stay another week, Honey," he urged afterward. "Don't leave me yet."

"I can't."

"Yes, you can. Call Mac. He'll look out for things for you. Just one more week."

Because she wanted to be with him as much as he wanted to be with her, she agreed. Another week and then she'd leave.

That first party opened the floodgates to invitations. Beau sorted through them, along with the phone calls, and only chose the ones he believed would do the most for his career and still take the least amount from their time alone together.

Honey checked the pile of mail and phone messages with a sinking heart. Every time the phone rang it was like a death knell.

During the day, Beau was busy with several different projects: publicity interviews, memorizing lines for the show, meetings with directors and producers, photographic sessions. By the time he came home in the late afternoon, he was so exhausted they would eat dinner, read to Meagan and then curl up together and watch TV or give up and begin another late-evening round of parties, clubs and publicity shots.

The first episode was due to premiere in two weeks, and all the socializing was designed to promote the new "star" of the show. Beau had already promised to do whatever was necessary as long as his part was finished by the time the one-hour pilot hit the airwaves. It was something they both knew he had to do until he was big enough to say no, but that didn't make it any easier.

"Let's just make an appearance and get out of there," Beau said one night as she redid his tie. "I'm damn sick and tired of all this running around. I've turned down three parties this week, and if this one wasn't for a good producer, I'd cancel."

Honey's heart lifted with his grumbling words. Her mouth only uttered three words. "I'd love that."

His green eyes burned with a desire that was becoming easy to detect, but which never failed to light a brushfire inside her. His look told her of his love and the deep need he had for her. She answered silently, her body swaying toward his, her fingers splaying across his broad chest. For a moment his hands clenched her hips, drawing her closer, but then reluctantly he released her. He gave a lopsided grin. "We'd better leave right now, before I change my mind."

She nodded, unable to speak. Plucking her small black purse from the bed as she left the room, she sighed to herself.

As they drove away she practiced the smile she knew she would be expected to wear, but Beau's knowing look told her he saw the small difference— the fact that her eyes and soul weren't smiling with her mouth.

They took the freeway north, but after a few miles they exited onto a narrow, winding road lit only by the full moon. It wasn't until they turned onto another road that Honey really looked out the window and noticed the scenery. "How odd," she said, more to herself than to Beau as her eyes darted along the roadside.

"What is?"

"This area. It reminds me a little of my farm," she answered absently.

"A little bit of Texas in Southern California?" he teased her gently, hiding the ache her comment had created. Texas. She always seemed to be comparing the two and California never won.

The party was at a small ranch house with a large patio that disappeared into the darkness. The trees in the backyard held strings of twinkling white lights on their branches that made Honey think of Christmas. The same crowd was there, with a different cast of producers, directors and actors. The painful rounds of introductions began all over again.

They stayed for an hour, until Beau claimed a headache and they left, Honey giggling because of his unoriginal line. "Couldn't you have come up with a better one than that?"

His hand was possessive as he dragged her back to the car, a grin creasing his face. "I'm paid to act, not to write."

"In case you didn't notice, my darling Beau, people were looking at you a little strangely. They expected you to say I had the headache, not you."

"Did you?" He paused in front of the car door, hesitating as he stared down at her, his green eyes searching her face. She couldn't deny it. "I might have if we hadn't got out of there when we did."

He opened the door and let her slide in. "That's what I thought," he muttered as he shut her door and walked around to the driver's side.

The trip home was placid, a peaceful kind of quiet that allowed the soft music they were listening to to wash away any disquieting thoughts.

Honey began to hum along with the radio, which was playing an old movie song that always brought a sweetness to her mood.

"Honey."

"Hmm?" Her hand was coiled lightly in his, the feel of his warm flesh like a bond, connecting each to the other.

"After the series starts, the pace won't be this hectic. You know that, don't you?"

Honey nodded, although part of her didn't quite believe him.

"I'll also have time to look around for a larger house, one that suits our needs rather than just filling the bill for the moment."

"Yes," she whispered, dreading what was coming, yet knowing the conversation had been postponed long enough.

"If everything works out, will you come live with me for a while? Try it out?"

"I can't." Her voice was hardly a whisper, her throat was so choked with the effort of her answer.

"Try," he said. "Just try."

She shook her head, unable to explain the panic she felt at giving up all that was familiar to her. She had done it once. She didn't think she could stand the pain of failing again.

"It beats the hell out of me how you can be such a fantastic lady in every way but one—you're as stubborn as hell, especially when it comes to that damned piece of ground of yours in Texas. It's not really another word for heaven, you know. It's just a label for another place to live."

She actually felt his patience snap, but the words he wanted to hear wouldn't form in her throat.

As if he had read her mind, he vented a great sigh, filling the car with an invisible depression. "Okay, okay. You're right. You can't."

They walked up the two steps to the front door, Beau's arm around her waist. She knew he wasn't really surprised by her refusal. He was sad, instead.

The front door flew opened, spilling light onto the steps. Shelly was in the entryway, her face ashen even in the dim light. "Beau," she began.

He stopped in his tracks, his body rigid. "What's wrong? Is it Meagan?"

Shelly shook her head "No, she's fine. But Pamela has been calling every hour since you left. She's been hurt in an auto accident. Her boyfriend was killed."

The expression on Beau's face was closed and blank. His hand tightened on Honey's waist. When he spoke, his voice was perfectly level. "Did she leave a number?"

Shelly's eyes were wide as she handed Beau the slip of paper clenched in her fist. "Yes, but—"

Beau's arm deserted Honey's waist as he reached for the crumpled paper. Suddenly Honey felt icy cold. The response was unreasonable under the circumstances, she knew, but she had felt unnoticed and unloved as soon as Pamela stepped back into the picture. She had had a premonition that the woman's association with Beau wasn't over, despite his denials. His reaction to Shelly's announcement verified it.

"Thanks, Shelly," he said absently, giving her shoulder a quick squeeze as he passed into the house.

Before Honey knew it, she and Shelly were alone in the hallway and Beau had quietly, but firmly, shut the study door.

"Texas..." Shelly began, then stopped. She cleared her throat and smiled timorously. "I seem to be starting a lot of sentences but not finishing them."

Honey smiled back, but her face felt as if it were about to crack. Beau had heard Pamela's name and gone running.

Shelly put her hand on Honey's arm. "Let's have a glass of wine," she said. "I could use a little something after three hours of Pamela's hysterics."

"Will she be all right?" Honey finally remembered to ask, following Shelly to the cart in the living room that served as a bar.

Shelly poured two glasses, handing one to Honey. "Both legs are broken, but her mouth is working as well as ever," she said dryly.

"She's got to be in a lot of pain," Honey replied automatically. She felt as if she were the one in shock. Her hands were freezing and her brain was numb.

"Pain is what Pamela has the talent to put other people through, not what she's suffering from."

Honey's eyes widened. She had never heard Shelly speak so callously before. "She's human, Shelly. She has to have some redeeming qualities."

"Don't ask me to recite them," Shelly retorted.

"She must have had enough for Beau to fall in love with her."

Shelly frowned into the glass in her hand. "Maybe. I guess there's no accounting for taste."

Honey winced. Even though she knew the facts, it still hurt. "And he must still love her. After all, she is the mother of his child," she said hollowly, rubbing salt into her own wound.

Shelly's green eyes rounded in surprise. "Beau might have been stupid once, Texas. But he learned his lesson."

The study door opened, and they both swiveled toward the living room entrance.

Beau stood there, his eyes shifting from Shelly to Honey. "I've got a flight to Brownsville that leaves in two hours. I'll be gone about three days," he said abruptly. "Please stay here, Honey. I'll call you as soon as I get things squared away. Okay?" Before either of them could answer, he was gone.

"I stand corrected," Shelly murmured under her breath, and the bruised look in Honey's eyes agreed.

Honey couldn't speak. She felt as if she were bleeding inside.

When he disappeared up the stairs, Honey sat down. She had never felt the excruciating pain of loving him as much as she did at that moment. Beau and Pamela had had a beautiful child together. They had a history, times of loving and laughing together. Honey's own period with him hadn't even lasted three months.

At last she walked up the stairs to her room. She'd pack and leave in the morning. There were others to comfort him, when and if he returned.

She hesitated for a moment outside his bedroom door, listening to drawers opening and closing as Beau quickly packed. Then she walked on to her own room. After a warm shower, Honey slipped into her favorite nightgown and slid between the sheets, turning out the light and waiting in the dark for Beau. Surely he would say goodbye to her.

An hour later she heard shuffling footsteps on the landing and tensed. But they passed her door, stopped for a beat, then continued to the stairs.

Then her tears began to flow.

EVERYTHING WAS PACKED and ready. He had fifteen minutes more before he had to leave.

Beau stood in the darkened center of his bedroom and stared at the only light source in the room—the street lamp outlining the window. He turned his back on the view, and sat on the side of his bed holding his head in his hands.

Pamela. During the past four years he had cursed her, loved her and laughed and cried with her. In the beginning he had fallen in love with her, and at the end he had known that he could never really have loved her, only the ghost of what he thought she had been. What he had fallen in love with was a figment of his own imagination.

As a result, he had never felt so guilty about anything in his whole life.

At best, he had given her only the tiniest part of himself and had hoped it would be enough. At worst, he had ignored her completely.

He had made lots of mistakes in his life—hell, probably hundreds—but this one needed looking at closely if he was to continue with any other relationships that mattered to him. Especially with Honey.

He piled his pillows against the headboard and leaned back, staring at the ceiling as thoughts he had tried too long to repress began tumbling out of the messy files of his memory.

He had tried to change Pamela into what he had thought she should be instead of paying attention to what she was. Good Lord! He had been young, smug, and oh, so knowing! How cocky youth was.

Was he making the same mistake again? Did he ever do that with Meagan or Shelly? Always holding back a small part of himself?

He closed his eyes at that thought. Deep down, he knew he gave Meagan everything he could of himself: his laughter and his love as well as his strength and his weaknesses.

He had shared everything with Shelly, too. Now she was mature enough to make it on her own.

But Honey? There he wasn't so sure. Did he reserve a portion of himself from her? Ashamed, he knew the answer. Yes. His hands clutched at the comforter. He was bitterly afraid. There was so much going against their love, such as her need to hold on to something stable in her land. Was he being as selfish with Honey as he had been with Pamela?

He wasn't sure, and the not knowing was even more frightening. He wanted to say and do all the right things with Honey, but he wasn't sure what they were. If she didn't love him enough, he knew he'd simply die for want of her. Even withholding vital pieces of himself, he was still more vulnerable with her than he had ever been with anyone.

He loved her, heart and soul, but he wasn't brave enough to pry a commitment from her because he was more afraid of her rejection than he was of going on with the relationship as it was....

Apart.

His lids were drooping wearily as he stood up and reached for his suitcase. He wanted to be in Honey's bed, holding her, feeling the completeness he always felt when he was near her. But before he could do that, he had to get Pamela out of his life once and for all. No other solution was fair to Honey.

God, he was scared. He had been asking her to sacrifice her land and her solitude when all he had given her in return was his love. It wasn't much of a bargain.

10

AFTER TWO WEEKS of walking her property, Honey could finally breathe slowly enough to think rationally. As soon as she had got home, she had plunged back into her routine as if there were nothing she would rather be doing. But her body had been numbed against feeling and her brain anesthetized by self-induced novocaine. It was all a lie.

She had stayed at Beau's house two more days after he'd left, hoping against hope that he would call her with the reassurance that her fragile ego demanded. When no call had come, she'd known she'd lost him. He had been to see Pamela and had fallen in love with her again. So consuming was his renewed passion, he couldn't waste time calling her. She had left early on the third morning, despite Shelly's protests, returning to her farm late that afternoon.

Two days after she'd got home, Beau had finally got in touch with her. As soon as she'd heard his voice, she'd hung up the phone. She'd known that if she heard he was going back to Pamela, she would collapse. It was better this way, with her controlling her own future. He'd called four more times before he'd got the message. Even then her tears hadn't come. She was like a hollow shell, with nothing left to feel.

She was too proud to try to compete for a space in his heart, and she certainly wouldn't attempt to take Pamela's place.

But her home rang with loneliness. Meagan's and Beau's spirits were everywhere. Once, fixing herself a peanut butter and jelly sandwich, she had actually turned to ask Meagan if she would like one, too.

Twice, lying in bed in the middle of the night, she had rolled over and reached out for Beau, only to touch a cold, empty pillow. For the rest of the night she'd stared at the window-framed starry sky.

And every afternoon around six, she would sit immobilized, staring at the grounds. There was no special reason for the time of day, it just seemed that she was at her most vulnerable then. The slight low she usually experienced at dusk was magnified now beyond her comprehension. Deep depression had become her constant companion.

In reaction, she hid from life, staying on the farm, seeing no one. She knew what she was doing, too, and that made it all the worse, but she refused to delve into her feelings. She refused to think at all.

Every day her routine was the same. She woke up, ate and did her chores. Every morning by ten she was

at the computer, keeping up with the books she kept
for the local businesses. After a lunch she rarely did
more than toy with, she walked down the drive to her
mailbox. With monotonous regularity, all the mail
offered her was more receipts to post on accounts that
afternoon. Otherwise, she walked the property until
she had tired herself out enough to begin thinking of
the dark hours ahead without screaming her frustra-
tions into the empty silence of her life.

When the third week began, the routine was shat-
tered. As she opened the mailbox, a fat envelope con-
fronted her, Meagan's name above the return address.
Images and memories of the small girl spun through
her mind, images that hurt more than words could
say. Along with the thoughts of Meagan, sharp pictures of Beau intruded, which made the pain almost
unbearable.

Her hand froze, reaching for the envelope but not
quite touching it as she waited for the memories to
subside and take away at least some of her ache. But
they didn't. For an instant she even thought of leaving the letter there until later, but she knew it wouldn't
get any easier. Quickly Honey grabbed it, slamming
the mailbox shut, and began to walk back up the
driveway.

Seated at the kitchen table, she tore open the flap
and removed the contents. The three large pieces of

paper inside were finger-paint pictures of Honey, Beau, the hens and Sandals. Meagan, of course, played an important role in all of them, always holding Honey's hand.

A letter in Shelly's handwriting was enclosed. No salutation, just an indented first paragraph to mark the front page.

Meagan misses you very much, Texas. She talks about you as if you'll walk in the door any minute. And no one can speak to Beau without being snapped at. His new show premieres next Wednesday, and he's been working harder than he ever did in New York.

I'll be moving out next week. I found a job that thrills me, teaching learning-disabled children, and I know I'm going to love it.

Best to you. Beau hasn't been the same since you cut off communication with him. Can't you just speak to him on the phone? I think he needs you more than either of you know.

Love,

Shelly

Honey crossed her arms and laid her head down on the table with her eyes closed. Over and over, her

mind beat with the rhythm of the words. *I love him,
I love him.* And as the words thrummed in her blood-
stream, an overwhelming feeling of desolation swept
over her.

Beau had said he loved her, then he had asked her
to give up her land and her life in Texas to join him. It
would have been only her life that was altered. Not
his. Her stubborn pride whispered that it meant that
he cared less for her than she did for him. His experience with Pamela proved it, the voice insisted. Despite that, she had almost acquiesced.

Then Pamela entered the picture again, and everything had turned to ashes. He had run to her bedside,
leaving Honey behind so quickly her head had spun.

She couldn't bear the possibility that he had decided to take Pamela back. But he hadn't called again,
and that supported her belief, so she tried not to think
of it at all. She laughed bitterly, choking on the lump
caught in her throat. She had lost a fight she hadn't
even fought!

Her head came up, a dawning realization lighting
her eyes.

She had been isolated here for so long that licking
her wounds had become a habit, long after the loss of
Peter had healed. She had buried herself so deeply that
she had become petrified of venturing away. She

hadn't even tried to fight! She had become such a chicken that she wouldn't even attempt to win the man she loved!

The impact of the mess she had created, the depth of her sacrifice, hit her like a rocket. Stupid! She had opted for a piece of land over living a complete life with the man she loved. She had molded her ten acres into husband, confidant, friend. Even lover.

In the process, she had sacrificed family, friendship and happiness—a result that was as bland as death itself and nearly as final.

Stupid! Stupid! Her fist slammed the tabletop. She had been so childishly stupid!

Except for two disastrous years in the city, she had created a sanctuary here—a safe place where no one else could enter. But it was really a self-made prison. She had been grooming herself for a solitary life and hadn't even been aware of it. Her land was a great place to hide. But hiding wasn't living; it was existing. She had done that with Peter, too. Choosing everything except a complete commitment to him.

The arguments they had had came to mind, along with the accusations he had thrown at her, which had washed over her without hurting at the time. Now they had barbs that dug deep.

"You love this damned dirt better than you love me!" he had said disgustedly.

"It's my home," she had replied with a dignity that was funny now. So funny it was painful.

Home was a place where you were surrounded by people who loved you, not a particular dot on a map. It had nothing to do with geographic location; it was a state of mind, a feeling of warmth and completeness, not of solitude.

Home was wherever Beau and Meagan were, not a ranch that kept her away from life instead of reaching out for love and living.

She raised her chin with grim determination. She was better for Beau than Pamela could ever hope to be. For Meagan, too. She had more to offer them than any other woman could dream of. And she would fight for that right. Beau had been drawn to her in ways Pamela couldn't begin to understand. But Honey had two enemies—herself and the ghost of an old love. She knew she could handle the former, and she'd give the latter one a damned good fight!

Without further hesitation she walked over to the phone. Sniffing, she dialed a number and waited for it to be answered. She spoke huskily but with determination. "This is Honey Carter. I wonder if you could come out and give me an estimate on my property. I'm thinking of selling . . ."

BEAU SLAMMED THE CAR DOOR and walked toward the breezeway that connected to the house. It was almost seven o'clock in the evening, but it could have been midnight he was so worn out.

Slipping his key into the lock, he let himself into the empty kitchen, knowing dinner wouldn't be served tonight since it was the housekeeper's day off. The TV was blaring, telling him Meagan was watching her favorite show. Shelly was probably upstairs packing boxes. She was moving in the morning.

"Beau? Is that you?" Shelly called out as he walked toward the hall.

"Were you expecting someone else?" he asked, standing there, hands on hips, as he watched her peeking over the balcony. For a split second he remembered Honey doing the same thing, her smile brightening the tired end of the day and brushing his cobwebs away. Then came the stab of pain as he remembered she was gone. Forever.

"No," Shelly answered, a frown marring her brow and telling him he was revealing his black mood again. He tried to smile at her, but was sure the result resembled a grimace instead. "Your program comes on in half an hour, but there's time enough for you to eat the sandwich in the fridge."

"Thanks, but I'm not hungry," he said flatly, turning to join Meagan in the living room. Right now he desperately needed a hug from his daughter.

He needed Honey, too, but she had left him and his life, telling him silently that she wasn't ready to love him so fully that she would move. The first few days after he had got home from that whirlwind trip to Brownsville, he had reached for the phone to hear her soft Southern voice as if it were an addiction he couldn't control. But she wouldn't even speak to him.

He had waited for her to call and explain, but she never did. Since then he had cursed himself over and over. He had written letter after letter, but in the re-reading he realized how stiff and formal they were. All he really wanted to do was to tell her how much he loved and needed her.

She already knew that. He had said it so many times before. Obviously, if she hadn't contacted him, she didn't love him, so he'd stopped trying to reach her. Now it was a matter of pride. He'd be damned if he'd grovel!

He knew she'd been hurt by the way he had flown to Pamela's side, but she hadn't let him explain. It had taken a week to get Pamela to sign the papers and to have an injunction filed against her. She was never to go near Meagan again or she would be arrested for the kidnapping. It had taken all his concentration and a damned good lawyer to make sure the agreement was airtight and then signed when she was at her most vulnerable . . . in a hospital bed with bills that had to be paid if she was to get the treatment necessary to be whole again.

Pamela could never enter their lives again. But Honey wouldn't even listen to him.

With Honey gone, all the sunshine and sweetness was erased from his life, leaving behind a bitter, barren wasteland where his soul and heart had been.

What if someone else called her? He smiled genuinely for the first time in days. Maybe there was a way they could both keep their prides intact and still have another chance. It was worth a try.

HONEY SHOWERED, put on her robe and fixed a pot of tea. She got everything ready and sat down in front of the television, ready to watch the premiere of Beau's show.

In a way, she had pretended it was a date: showering, bath powder, a light dusting of makeup and then the pot of freshly brewed tea served in her best china. The preparations kept her busy and fended off the terrible knowledge that she had made an irreparable mistake, telling Beau by her silence that she had chosen the land, not him.

The theme music began, and Honey's eyes were fixed to the screen as it showed Beau in several different moments of peril: with a gun, jumping from roof to roof, standing over a dead body and finally one with him smiling at a beautiful woman hanging on his arm. He looked terrific in each scene.

Before the program was half over, Honey's tears were cascading down her cheeks. She'd wipe them away and more would appear. He was great, and she knew he'd be the newest sex symbol for millions of women across the country. Every little move he made inspired memories of their times together.

That night she didn't sleep at all.

By the next morning, her decision was made. She would swallow her pride and her fears. Instead of writing or calling, she would fly to California and confront Beau, face-to-face. With any luck she could convince him of her love.

Taking a deep breath, she steeled herself for the first step of her independence. Even the fear of Beau's rejection couldn't keep her from trying to prove to him that they belonged together. After all, what did she have to lose except a life of total loneliness, which would be there waiting, regardless?

She crossed her fingers and said a prayer.

Later that evening, when the phone rang, Honey was packing the crystal she had only used once—just another possession with invisible ties to the past and little worth in her life.

"Honey?" a woman said hesitantly.

"Shelly? Is that you? Is everything all right?"

"Well . . ." Shelly began.

"Is it Beau?" Honey's hands tightened on the receiver. Her heart fluttered rapidly from anxiety. "Or Meagan?"

"Both."

"Both what?" Her tension was obvious.

She heard Shelly take a deep breath. "Meagan is having a recital. She's playing Rapunzel at school, and Beau asked me to call and see if you would come out for it. She has her heart set on your being there. To tell you the truth, I think Beau does, too."

Honey's voice softened. "Really?"

"They love you, Texas," Shelly said honestly. "They miss you."

Honey hesitated a moment, then plunged ahead. "Is Beau still pining for her?"

"Pamela?" Utter surprise etched Shelly's voice. "He never loved her. I thought you knew that."

"But the night he found out . . ." Her voice faltered.

" . . . was terrible. Beau has more guilt feelings about that woman than the law allows. He's always felt he should have made her get help."

"Is she there?" Honey's fingers cluthced the phone again as she waited for the answer.

"Are you kidding?" Shelly exclaimed. "Honey," she began, patience threading her voice along with a faint lilt of laughter, "why don't you come out and ask Beau those questions? He's really the one who should answer them."

Honey's heart was pounding in her ears. This had been the chance she had wanted; only now that it was here, fear coursed through her body, making her knees tremble. But determination firmed her words—determination and a small glimmer of hope to which she clung. "I'll be there," she said resolutely. "When?"

Shelly gave her the information, and after a few parting words, hung up.

Honey closed her eyes and muttered a thank-you prayer. It had to have been divine intervention that caused Shelly to call, giving her the official excuse she needed to visit.

And she was going to make the best of it. The very best.

BEAU, IF YOU STILL WANT ME, I'm yours. No. *Beau, I realize now that I love you with all my heart and I want to live with you.* That wouldn't do, either. *Beau, did you mean that proposal?* Dumb!

None of her preplanned speeches sounded right.

As Honey slipped into the passenger seat of Beau's car, she eyed him carefully and wondered what to say. He had met her plane, spoken a calm hello, made a neutral comment on the weather and hadn't said a word since. The longer the silence continued, the more her heart raced.

So she simply waited him out, her eyes stealing sideways toward his profile as he backed out of the parking space. He was as devastatingly handsome as ever, only now there were shallow creases bordering his mouth that made his expression seem almost harsh. She gulped hard and broke the silence. After all, she didn't have anything to lose. "So, how has California been treating you?" she asked brightly.

"I love California," he replied evenly. "It's beautiful."

"That's nice."

"My career is doing very well, too, thank you."

She couldn't detect the relieved teasing in his voice. "Two wonderfuls," she said dryly, trying to decide if she had just played the part of the perfect fool.

"It's the perfect climate."

"Great."

She glanced out the window, noticing for the first time that they weren't taking the route she had remembered. "Where are we going? This isn't the way to your house, is it?"

He shook his head, staring straight ahead. "We've moved. It's just a little farther down the road," he said quietly.

Twenty minutes later Beau slowed the car, turning onto a well-graded dirt road that bore a new burntwood sign that read Albot Ranch.

Honey sat quietly, belying the tension that had her strung so tightly. She had caught him glancing her way once or twice, but she couldn't interpret the expression in his eyes, and that made her all the more unsure. Her heart was beating frantically against her breast.

"Here we are," he said as he slowed to take a bend in the road, then stopped.

She looked up, her expression turning from sad to stunned as she stared through the windshield.

A large, white, two-storied house sparkled like a jewel in the afternoon sun. A shady veranda wound around three sides, welcoming visitors with a promise of coolness. Gray shutters and the big front door were opened in welcome. Farther back, toward the sides of the house, were other well-kept buildings, but Honey paid little attention to them. All her attention was focused on the house itself. Five or six trees shaded parts of the roof and the lawn, promising cooling breezes even in the desert heat of Southern California's summers. The house could have been featured on the cover of any self-respecting home-and-garden magazine.

"What do you think?" His knuckles were white as his hands wrapped tightly around the steering wheel.

Tears shimmered in her brown eyes, and she sniffled. "It's beautiful, Beau."

He turned toward her, holly-green eyes searching hers. "Yes," he murmured slowly. "Really beautiful."

"You bought it?" Her voice sounded hollow.

Something she couldn't name glittered in his eyes before he reluctantly answered. "Yes."

"Meagan will love it."

"She already does. She's inside with our housekeeper now, getting the place ready so we can move in next week. Do you like it?"

She couldn't speak, the lump in her throat rendering her mute. So she nodded vigorously instead.

Slowly, like warm, spilled molasses, his smile spread and touched her heart, instantly warming it. He lowered his head and his lips brushed hers in a wisp of a kiss. But she wasn't content with such a brief touch and edged closer, aching to feel the strength of his body. Beau groaned as he wrapped his arms firmly around her, dragging her across the seat and onto his lap.

She heard the thump of the steering wheel as he pushed the lever that bounced it out of the way, then she wasn't aware of anything but the glory of his hard body close to hers. It had been so long.... Her tongue felt the strength of his own, and it stole her breath away as he plundered her mouth. Her hands strained at his shoulders, trying to force him closer, closer, and his own arms helped by tightening around her.

"I love you so much it hurts," he said, pulling away slightly to inhale the scent of her.

"I love you, too." Her voice was shy, but her hand strayed to his jaw, loving the texture of his newly shaved skin.

"I didn't know if I'd ever get you out here again, but I knew I had to have another chance to change your mind."

She chuckled. "You already had." Her features turned somber as she leaned back so she could study his face. "Beau, I put the farm up for sale."

His eyes closed for a moment, then opened to stun Honey with their emerald brilliance. "Thank God," he said quietly. "But why?"

"Because I knew when I got back that I had made the wrong decision. The land wasn't what was important to me, not really. But your love was. I need you and Meagan far more than I need ten acres of dirt. Even before Shelly called, I was getting ready to come out here. I was ready to fight for you if I had to," she admitted, a small smile dimpling one cheek in the way he loved so much.

His body relaxed as if he had just taken a powerful tranquilizer. "It's nice to know where I rate in your priorities," he teased, eyes shining with a magical inner glow.

Honey's eyes didn't smile back. "Yes, it is, isn't it?"

Suddenly Beau's somber look matched hers. "Honey, all my life I've worked to reach this point in my career. If you only knew how close I came to dumping it all when you left—but I can't. I have Meagan to care for, and acting is all I really know how to do."

"I know." Better yet, she finally understood. Everything.

"Did you ever doubt it that I need you so bad it hurts?" he asked.

"For what?" She had to ask. She had to know that she was making the right choice, that she wasn't just being used as a substitute for all the others in his home life.

He couldn't have read her mind more clearly. He leaned away, framing her face with his strong hands. "Let's get a few things straight," he said determinedly. "I *don't* need you to be a housekeeper. I have one, and she's very good. I *don't* need you to be a mother to Meagan. Although she doesn't have one, I haven't done such a bad job with her. I *don't* need you to keep my appointments or be my social hostess. From now on I won't be doing much entertaining or spending so much time being entertained."

He stared at her, his green eyes hinting at thoughts she could only guess at. "What I do need is simply . . . you. Your softness, your common sense, your lively conversation." His tender smile deepened, and her pulse rocketed.

"But I also need your love like I need air to breathe. I love you, Honey Carter. I don't want to be without you. I don't want to turn over in the night and find you're not there. I don't want to hear something funny, or special, or heartbreaking, and not have you to share it with." His arms tightened around her. "I need to have you with me. To love you. To be with you."

"What about Pamela?" she asked softly, gathering the nerve at last to talk about the other woman with the person she had once mattered most to.

He sighed and leaned his head back against the headrest. "I only had two hours to get the wheels rolling. Pamela had to stay in the hospital, where she was, and I had to find an attorney who would tie her up legally so she could never be a threat to Meagan or us again." He looked at Honey, his green eyes softened with tenderness. "But I have the feeling that you didn't understand anything about that at all. Time was the main factor I was fighting against."

"But that night." Honey hesitated.

His eyes darkened. "I really needed to think about us. And what we were doing to each other. I didn't want to make the same mistake."

She forced a smile through teary eyes. "I'm yours, Beau, if you still want me," she said quietly, promising.

Once more he closed his eyes, this time in gratitude. "Thank goodness." As his arms tightened, she pulled away.

"On two conditions," she interjected, the smile stiff on her lips, doubt showing in her eyes.

"Name them," he said, promptly.

"First, I want to continue my accounting practice. I'm sure I can do as well here as I did in Texas."

"Done. In fact, there's a small office off the sitting room that's perfect for it. What else?"

"Who are the Albots? What did they raise here? Hens? Cattle? Horses? I want to have animals around."

He grinned broadly, deep satisfaction glowing all around him. "That's my name for this ranch. It's really initials. They stand for 'A Little Bit of Texas.' The people who lived here before didn't raise anything— it was their retreat, a summer place. But you can raise anything you please—hens and cattle, kittens and children. It doesn't matter to me as long as you're so happy you'll never leave me again."

A small sigh escaped her. "Kittens and children sound wonderful," she said, wondering how she could ever have chosen anything above him. He was everything she had ever wanted. Everything and more.

Then her thoughts were interrupted by the fulfilled promise of his kiss.

RUGGED. SEXY. HEROIC.

OUTLAWS *and* HEROES

Stony Carlton—A lone wolf determined never to be
tied down.

Gabriel Taylor—Accused and found guilty by
small-town gossip.

Clay Barker—At Revenge Unlimited, he *is* the law.

JOAN JOHNSTON, DALLAS SCHULZE and
MALLORY RUSH, three of romance fiction's
biggest names, have created three unforgettable
men—modern heroes who have the courage to fight
for what is right....

OUTLAWS AND HEROES—available in September
wherever Harlequin books are sold.

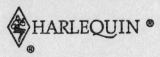 HARLEQUIN ®

MILLION DOLLAR SWEEPSTAKES (III)

HARLEQUIN®

Temptation®

Secret Fantasies

Do you have a secret fantasy?

Kasey Halliday does—she's fallen hard for the "boy" next door. Will Eastman is sexy, sophisticated and definitely interested in Kasey. But there's a mysterious side to this man she can't quite fathom. Find out what Will is hiding in #554 STRANGER IN MY ARMS by Madeline Harper—available in September 1995.

Everybody has a secret fantasy. And you'll find them all in Temptation's exciting new yearlong miniseries, Secret Fantasies. Beginning January 1995, one book each month focuses on the hero's or heroine's innermost romantic desires....

SF-9

MOVE OVER, MELROSE PLACE!

> Apartment for rent
> One bedroom
> Bachelor Arms
> 555-1234

Come live and love in L.A. with the tenants of Bachelor Arms. Enjoy a year's worth of wonderful love stories and meet colorful neighbors you'll bump into again and again.

Startling events from Bachelor Arms' past return to stir up scandal, heartache and painful memories for three of its tenants. Read popular Candace Schuler's three sexy and exciting books to find out how passion, love and betrayal at Bachelor Arms affect the lives of three dynamic men. Bestselling author of over fifteen romance novels, Candace is sure to keep you hooked on Bachelor Arms with her steamy, sensual stories.

LOVERS AND STRANGERS #549 (August 1995)

SEDUCED AND BETRAYED #553 (September 1995)

PASSION AND SCANDAL #557 (October 1995)

Next to move into Bachelor Arms are the heroes and heroines in books by ever-popular Judith Arnold!

Don't miss the goings-on at Bachelor Arms

As a *Privileged Woman,* you'll be entitled to all these *Free Benefits.* And *Free Gifts,* too.

To thank you for buying our books, we've designed an exclusive FREE program called *PAGES & PRIVILEGES™.* You can enroll with just one Proof of Purchase, and get the kind of luxuries that, until now, you could only read about.

*B*IG HOTEL DISCOUNTS

A privileged woman stays in the finest hotels. And so can you—at up to 60% off! Imagine standing in a hotel check-in line and watching as the guest in front of you pays $150 for the same room that's only costing you $60. Your *Pages & Privileges* discounts are good at Sheraton, Marriott, Best Western, Hyatt and thousands of other fine hotels all over the U.S., Canada and Europe.

*F*REE DISCOUNT TRAVEL SERVICE

A privileged woman is always jetting to romantic places. When <u>you</u> fly, just make one phone call for the lowest published airfare at time of booking—<u>or double the difference back!</u> PLUS—

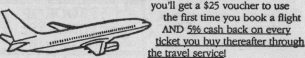

you'll get a $25 voucher to use the first time you book a flight AND <u>5% cash back on every ticket you buy thereafter through</u> <u>the travel service!</u>

𝓕REE GIFTS!

A privileged woman is always getting wonderful gifts.
Luxuriate in rich fragrances that will stir your senses (and his). This gift-boxed assortment of fine perfumes includes three popular scents, each in a beautiful designer bottle. <u>Truly Lace</u>...This luxurious fragrance unveils your sensuous side. <u>L'Effleur</u>...discover the romance of the Victorian era with this soft floral. <u>Muguet des bois</u>...a single note floral of singular beauty.

𝓕REE INSIDER TIPS LETTER

A privileged woman is always informed. And you'll be, too, with our free letter full of fascinating information and sneak previews of upcoming books.

𝓜ORE GREAT GIFTS & BENEFITS TO COME

A privileged woman always has a lot to look forward to. And so will you. You get all these wonderful FREE gifts and benefits now with only one purchase...and there are no additional purchases required. However, each additional retail purchase of Harlequin and Silhouette books brings you a step closer to even more great FREE benefits like half-price movie tickets... and even more FREE gifts.

L'Effleur...This basketful of romance lets you discover L'Effleur from head to toe, heart to home.

Truly Lace...
A basket spun with the sensuous luxuries of Truly Lace, including Dusting Powder in a reusable satin and lace covered box.

Complete the Enrollment Form
in the front of this book and
mail it with this Proof of Purchase.

PROOF OF PURCHASE
Offer expires October 31, 1996

WL-PP4